South He

"Refreshing sur
journey of makin̟ ... . -
suspense; Enjoyable from start to finish."
Colleen Munson, Western Michigan University Head Volleyball Coach, 2014 MAC Coach of the Year.

"This book feels like summer! You can almost smell the tanning lotion and taste the ice cream. Great beach read. Flirtatious fun among teens turns into regret, causing us to explore the 'common denominator' threaded throughout the story…choices. In the end, it's the choices we make that affect us all."
Susan K. Flach, Author of *A Song and a Seashell* (Young Adult Romance Series).

"*South Heaven* is more than a great story; it challenges the reader to reflect and consider how to live for what matters most."
Tim Hiller, Author of *Strive*, Western Michigan University Football Player (QB), Wuerffel Trophy recipient (Humanitarian Heisman),

"This is a well-written book that I had a hard time putting down. It took me back to my younger days of playing volleyball on the sands of South Haven. Jerry does an excellent job of keeping your interest with the trials and tribulations that teens and young adults face today. Reconfirming that when facing challenges and obstacles in your life; keeping true to your faith, values and beliefs will keep you on the right path."
Vicky Groat, St. Philip Varsity Volleyball Coach, Ten Michigan High School State Championships.

"*South Heaven* is an enjoyable read that is action packed with real life characters and struggles. Relatable to both teens and adults, this book offers opportunities for personal reflection and depicts the impact our choices have in life. Full of suspense, witty humor, athletics, romance and a Christian worldview, this is a read one can't put down." **Taria Moser, Calhoun Christian School (CCS) Varsity Volleyball Coach, Spring Arbor Volleyball Player.**

"Jerry Lambert creates a vivid picture of the obstacles and choices that not only athletes face but all young people in today's society trying to stay true to their faith and themselves. It was packed with anticipation, romance and thrill! Great read, I couldn't put it down!" **Lena Oliver, Western Michigan Volleyball Player, MAC Defensive Player of the Year, 2x Cobra Magazine National Defensive Player of the Year, 4 High School State Championships.**

"Jerry Lambert's choice of South Haven for the setting of his newest book, *South Heaven*, is fitting. Readers of *South Heaven* will quickly identify with the attractions that lure visitors to this lakeshore community — sandy beaches, Lake Michigan, quaint downtown and colorful, sunsets. But as the book's college-age characters — Mickey, Josie, Jack and Jerrid — find out, pursuing the many summer pleasures offered in a beachtown can bring about grave consequences."
Becky Burkert-Kark, Editor, *South Haven Tribune*

"Jerry Lambert has crafted an enjoyable tale with interesting characters in a vivid, beautiful setting that can be read in a couple of sittings. Young girls and guys alike will get into and be able to really relate to at least one of the major characters. It's a story of choices and consequences and will make the readers think about choices they are facing, or will be facing, in their lives. Great book to stir conversation with sports teams, youth groups or your own kids."
Mike McGeath, Fellowship of Christian Athletes (FCA) Regional Director, Volleyball Coach at Heritage Christian High School, Western Michigan University Football Player.

SOUTH HEAVEN

By:

JERRY LAMBERT

Published by Big Mac Publishers
Kingston, TN 37763

Copyright

Copyright © 2016 by Jerry Lambert All rights reserved. Written permission must be secured from the publisher or author to use or reproduce any part of this book, except for brief quotations in critical reviews or articles.

Author:	Jerry Lambert
Editor:	Tiffany Jones
All photos except where noted:	Copyright © 2016 Jerry Lambert
Cover photographs, Author photo:	Michelle Lambert
Formatting:	Michelle Lambert

Library of Congress Control Number: 2016945222
Library of Congress subject headings suggestions:

1. Christian Fiction--Contemporary
2. Christian Romance -- Contemporary
3. Christian Fiction – Other
4. Christian Fiction – Family
5. Christian Fiction – Action & Adventure

BISAC Classification Suggestions:

1. FIC002000   FICTION / Action & Adventure
2. FIC042040   FICTION / Christian / Romance
3. FIC043000   FICTION / Coming of Age
4. FIC042000   FICTION / Christian / General

ISBN-13 for Black and White Paperback: 978-1-937355-25-8   V: 1.0
ISBN-13 for eBook: 978-1-937355-26-5

To purchase additional copies of *South Heaven* or to learn more about the author go to (**https://www.facebook.com/jerrylambertauthor**) or his author page on Amazon.com.

Other terrific books by Jerry & bestsellers in their class: *Trophy White Tales, The Hunting Spirit, & North of Wrong.* from Jerry or Amazon & other vendors.

Big Mac Publishers, Kingston, TN 37763
Written and processed in the United States of America

Table of Contents

Acknowledgements

I wish to extend my heartfelt gratitude to the following people for their helpful contributions towards the development of *South Heaven*. I greatly appreciated the input and inspiration that came from the first readers who read pre-published drafts. This list includes Connie Crofoot, Jeralyn Belote, Gayle Walton, Nicole Corstange, and Michelle Lambert. In addition, I want to thank Tiffany Jones for contributing with her talented editing skills.

Once again, I was able to design the book's cover with the aid of Michelle Lambert, Lindsey Barry and Greg McElveen's technical skills. Greg continues to provide valuable insight and words of wisdom considering all the things needed for book publishing.

South Heaven is set in South Haven, Michigan, a small coastal town that sits along the sandy shores of Lake Michigan. I have visited this popular destination quite often. I've played beach volleyball, biked the Kal-Haven trail, caught big silver fish, dined on perch, ate ice cream, walked the peer and seen numerous sunsets. For the record, they are simply spectacular. I want to thank Almighty God, the Creator for gifting us this little piece of heaven on earth and for allowing me the opportunity of introducing it to others through the world of words.

Chapter One

Sunlight dances on the water while white-capped waves brilliantly crash ashore. A cool morning breeze blows gently from the magnificent Great Lake known as Lake Michigan. Mickey's tanned bare feet rhythmically pound the sand maintaining a timed beat. Twenty-one year old Mikayla McPherson, a.k.a. Mickey, runs the beach as part of her ongoing conditioning program. Running in the sand builds endurance, strengthens the legs and invigorates the spirit. Mickey's bleach blond ponytail bobs back and forth across her athletic sculpted back as if it is keeping time to the loud music pumping into her ears. Jamie Grace sings *Beautiful Day* to finish the playlist on her iPod that's simply labeled "Run." Mickey can't think of any other place that she would rather be.

Two years ago, Mickey was awarded the prestigious title of Michigan's Miss Volleyball after leading her Christian High School team to a State Championship. The trophy is given to the premier high school player in the state of Michigan as voted on by the sporting press. A lot of hard work earned her the award, and she keeps pressing on to maintain a peak physical fitness level. She is now preparing for her junior season at Michigan State University where she is expected, as team captain, to lead her team to a conference and possibly a national championship. High expectations have once again been placed on the talented athlete and she is vigorously working towards her goals.

To know Mickey is to like Mickey. She doesn't let her exceptional volleyball skills solely identify her. She has an exuberant personality and a caring heart. Talk about a zest for life. Younger girls strive to imitate her. A finer role model would be hard to find.

The sun has risen announcing another glorious morning. Seagulls scatter as the young athlete completes her three mile run. On top of a bluff overlooking the Great Lake sits a small white cottage that is owned by Mickey's Aunt Connie. Connie has invited her niece to stay with her over the summer to help her with the gallery that she owns in downtown South Haven. Mickey embraces the opportunity. Connie has always been her kindred spirit and the two share a deep bond. Both are artistic and seek out adventure. In previous years Mickey and her family would take a two-week vacation here. The family jokingly nicknamed the coastal paradise South Heaven. If there was ever a heaven on earth, then it would definitely be here.

South Haven is a small town in southern Michigan that caters to the tourists who seek out all the treats that a quaint coastal town has to offer. Sun, sand, boats, shopping, fine dining, ice cream parlors and a feel good atmosphere make it a destination retreat for people living in northern Indiana and southern Michigan. A fair share of the visitors, also venture up from Chicago, Illinois.

South Haven was founded in 1787 by Ottawa, Miami and Potawatomi tribes who called the area "Ni-Ko-Nong" which translates into English as "beautiful sunsets." J.R. Monroe came here during the pioneer times and settled the area with the opening of sawmills. The quality lumber was shipped across Lake Michigan to ports in Chicago and Milwaukee. After the land was cleared, fruit farmers moved in and developed prosperous peach, apple, and blueberry farms. In 1969, South Haven was titled the World's Blueberry capital.

Mickey's family resides in Battle Creek, Michigan, otherwise known as *Cereal City*. The city is only an hour and a half drive inland to the southeast. Mickey's dad works for the world famous Kellogg Company; home of Tony the Tiger and Toucan Sam. Wherever the wind is right, you can smell the wonderful aroma of sweetened cereal in the air.

Mickey pulls her white and green MSU shirt up over her head and throws it into the sand along with her Spartan green Nike running shorts. She then places her iPod and ear buds on top of her small pile of clothes. Next, the swimsuit clad beauty high steps it into the incoming tide and quickly dives under the clear cold water. The drastic change in temperature jolts her entire being, and the baptism vigorously lets her know that she is indeed alive!

When Mickey emerges from the blue H2O, her sun kissed skin glistens. She feels like a fairytale princess jeweled in nature's splendor. Being single, she naturally wonders if she will ever meet someone and start a relationship. Attracting boys has never been the problem. Mickey's concern is finding the right one who will like her for who she is and not just for how she looks.

With no towel immediately handy, Mickey must drip dry. Fortunately, the sun has risen high enough to make this process quick. Sand cakes onto her wet feet as she walks the beach towards the hill that she must climb to reach Connie's cottage.

Exactly one hundred wood steps lead up to the back deck. The west winds have sandblasted the boards smooth and are not a problem for the bare feet that traverse up and down them. Waiting on the deck with a fresh glass of orange juice is Connie and her German shepherd, Sadie. Connie looks up over the top of her reading glasses and smiles at Mickey as she closes her Bible. Then, in typical Aunt Connie fashion, she stands up, gazes out over the Great Lake and exclaims, "This is the day that the Lord has made." Then in unison Connie and Mickey say together, "Let us be glad and rejoice in it!" Life is good.

Mickey runs off to take a quick shower to prepare for her day at the gallery. At 9:40 a.m., the ladies climb aboard Cannondale mountain bikes for the short ride to work. Connie is two decades older than her niece but maintains the fitness lifestyle that so many of the townspeople keep. She is rather eccentric, and eccentric people are drawn to lake living.

At precisely 10 a.m., Connie flips the front door sign to read *open*. As she performs this task, two fire trucks roar past with their lights flashing and sirens blaring. Loud sirens are an uncommon sound in this small community, and the noise shatters the usual tranquil atmosphere. As soon as the two red trucks disappear, an ambulance follows along the exact same route.

The sirens and flashing lights are quickly forgotten when a married couple from Chicago walk through the front door.

"Good morning and welcome to Great Lake Expressions," says the happy store owner. "How can I help you?"

The wife replies, "Hello, my name is Jacqui Reece and this is my husband, Brian. We recently purchased a condominium along the lake and are in need of a large picture to hang in our living room."

"Do you have anything specific in mind?"

"I am looking for something that showcases South Haven's wonderful sunsets."

"You've picked the right place. We have quite a selection. Please follow me."

Connie leads them to the wall that displays a variety of sunsets. The couple is excited about their new condominium that they have purchased. They have bought the place to use as a summer retreat from Brian's stressful job as a stock broker and Jaqui's work as an interior designer. Mickey sees that they are interested in a limited edition print of one of her paintings. Connie winks at her niece as she removes the framed picture from the wall and walks it over to the cash register. Mickey is feeling good about her decision to work at the gallery. South Haven is looking like a modern-day promised land. Time will tell.

Chapter 2

Jack buckles the strap on his helmet and looks at his buddy and says, "Are you ready, Alice?"

"Who are you calling Alice, Nancy-boy?" replies Jerrid as he straddles his bike.

Jack Thayer and his best friend, Jerrid Stone, start pedaling their mountain bikes down the Kal-Haven Trail. Heavily muscled from countless hours of pushing weight, biking helps to keep them lean and builds up their lung capacity. Both men love the outdoors and workout outside as much as possible. The focus of this ride is to work on their endurance. The two buff competitors start off with a fast pace and push each other to excellence.

The Kal-Haven Trail is part of the Rails-to-Trails Conservancy that takes former railroad passages and converts them into riding and running trails. Thousands of fitness-minded people take to the trail throughout the year. The Kal-Haven Trail links the city of Kalamazoo to the small town of South Haven. The two 21-year-olds started in Kalamazoo, which happens to be the birth-home of the world famous Gibson guitars and Shakespeare fishing rods. They will finish their ride thirty-five miles later in the town of South Haven. Although they will pass quite a few people along the way, nobody on the trail has the ability to pass them.

Jack and Jerrid have been best friends for as long as they can remember and they both play football for the popular University of Michigan Wolverines. Both boys are projected to start for the Big-Ten powerhouse. Jerrid will begin his second year as the starting inside linebacker, and Jack has been chosen to lead the offense as the starting quarterback. He started the last five games the previous year and led the team to a 4 -1 record over that time frame.

Jack chose Michigan because of their strong tradition of building National Football League caliber quarterbacks. A long list of the University's quarterbacks have gone on to start in the NFL including Chad Henne, Jim Harbaugh, Todd Collins, Elvis Grbac, Brian Griese and arguably one of the best to ever don a football uniform, Tom Brady. Brady has since won numerous Super Bowl titles and is Jack's all-time favorite player. To literally follow in his hero's footsteps is something he does not take casually. Jack is honored to have this opportunity and is determined to make the most of it. Working out with Jerrid has been very beneficial. The linebacker is equally determined to excel. That makes for a good partnership.

Conversation bounces back and forth between the two men about the upcoming fall football season and the summer fun of pursuing beautiful beach babes. Expectations are always high at U of M, and these two carry most of the weight on their shoulders because of the positions that they play. Girls, sun and fun are expected to get them through the summer. The men have worked hard on their bodies through weightlifting and diet and they are anxious to show off their hard work to the ladies at the beach. Jack prefers blonds, and Jerrid prefers brunettes, but neither will discriminate if a girl is *hot*!

These two young athletes are also manly men who crave adventure. They spend a lot of time talking about the sporting life which includes previous hunting and fishing excursions. The boys are as passionate about the outdoors as they are about football; maybe even more so.

A velvet antlered buck crosses the trail in front of them. "How cool is that?" asks Jack.

"Very cool," Jerrid responds. "Man, that brings back memories."

"It sure does. I shot that tall-tined 10-point on Thanksgiving Day, and then you shot a big 8-point on Black Friday."

"Yeah, that feat is going to be hard to beat."

"I really want to go out west and hunt elk."

"You and me both; that is my dream hunt."

Both of the boys have dreams of pursuing Rocky Mountain elk and Alaskan moose in the near future. Surprisingly, these two sportsmen even skipped the traditional spring break hotspots to go turkey hunting with a teammate on his family's property in southern Georgia. The outdoor life is something that both of these twenty-one year olds crave. In essence, it helps to define them. It's part of their identity.

If these two men were responsible for writing a dictionary, the word *summer* would be defined as *fishing season*. The anglers have spent many summer days fishing a variety of lakes and rivers in southern Michigan. They have also spent a fair amount of time on Lake Michigan running down-riggers for salmon with a former high school teammate and his dad. This experience has led them to their upcoming summer job.

8

In 1966, Coho and Chinook salmon were introduced into Lake Michigan to promote sport fishing. People pay good money for this open water adventure. The average adult Great Lake Coho salmon weighs eight pounds, whereas the Chinook, otherwise named the King Salmon, average a weight of 30 - 40 pounds and 38 inches in length.

A U of M alumnus has hired the two men to run his charter fishing boat, The Wolverine, which docks at the marina in South Haven. Part of the deal is that they also get to live in the man's guest house. The party pad has two small bedrooms, a bathroom, a kitchen area and all-purpose room with a seventy inch flat screened television and pool table. To pay for rent, they are to mow the small accompanying lawn once a week and maintain the pool.

When the boys finally exit the bike trail into the sleepy streets of South Haven, they are forced to stop along the narrow road to allow two fire trucks to speed past them. Before they can continue on, an ambulance races past in fast pursuit. The adventurous youth decide to prolong their ride and follow the emergency vehicles.

After a mile, the two bicyclists observe a billow of black smoke rising above the sugar maple trees. Another two miles down the road they see flashing red lights. Firefighters are battling a blazing fire that has encompassed two homes. One home is already leveled to the ground and debris is scattered everywhere. It looks like a bomb went off!

A police officer arrives and immediately starts to scream at people, "Move back!"

As the crowd retreats they see a fireman exit the second house carrying a young child in his arms. He places what looks like an elementary aged girl on a stretcher, and the paramedics quickly wheel her away to the safety of their rig.

Another fireman comes out of the grey cloud of smoke carrying a young woman who is coughing profusely. He lays her on another stretcher and prepares to load her into a second ambulance. The lady panics and yells out, "Where is my baby? Is my baby girl ok?"

A paramedic assures the woman that her daughter has been rescued, and as a precaution they have already taken her to the hospital. Instantly relieved, the lady rests her head on the gurney, and the attendants load her into the ambulance.

The policeman has now successfully moved everybody back to a safe distance. Various people start asking the obvious, "What happened?"

A thin woman, wearing cut-off jean shorts, a faded stars and stripes patterned bikini bathing suit top and cheap flip-flops puffs on a cigarette and declares, "I'll tell you what happened. The idiot was cooking meth and blew himself up. It doesn't surprise any of us who live out here. You could tell that the guy was a meth head. His teeth were rotted out, and he was always tweakin. Unfortunately, the explosion set the house next to his on fire and it looks like the lady who recently moved in got hurt right along with her child."

"Who is she?" ask another woman wearing faded jeans and a white tank top.

"No one knows. She just moved in last Friday. Hopefully she will be ok. Such a shame," With this being said, the lady flicks her cigarette to the ground and smashes it with her thin sandal. A young child wearing nothing but a diaper comes running up to her. She picks the child up and walks back to her own home holding the baby on her hip.

Jack and Jerrid feel numb. Seeing the damage live and in color is a lot different than watching a local news report on TV. They silently climb back on their bikes and slowly head back toward town. After pedaling for a spell, Jerrid says, "That was a total buzz kill."

Jack bluntly replies, "No doubt, that was terrible."

The two boys had haughty visions of living the high life at this coastal paradise, and now this incident jolts them back to reality. Bad things can happen anywhere. Listening to the mother yell out for her baby girl really pulled at the heart strings. The bravery of the firefighters is not lost on them. "How heroic was that?" Jack thinks to himself, "I don't know if I would have the courage to enter a burning house to save someone that I am not connected to." He then thinks about the irony of the world. Jack is applauded by literally 100,000 screaming fans for throwing a football and playing a game. These guys risk their lives to save lives, and except for an occasional newspaper article, it is almost just considered another day at the job.

With just under a mile to go, Jerrid changes the mood by quickly racing out in front and yelling back over his shoulder, "Race you back into town." Jack shifts down into a lower gear and powers down in hot pursuit.

Chapter 3

Great Lake Expressions opened seven years ago. The gallery is a visual feast for the eyes. It features photographs that Connie has taken over the last several years of popular Lake Michigan sites. Included in her collection are several from Sleeping Bear Dunes National Park. ABC's *Good Morning America* declared this spot as the "Most beautiful place in America."

Connie photoshops her work by placing Bible scripture or inspiring quotes on her photographs and sells them at the gallery. Her bestselling piece is a photo that she took from her back deck during a sailor's red sunset. Accompanying this photo is the ever popular verse, *"From the rising of the sun to the place where it sets, the name of the LORD is to be praised,"* Psalm 113:3.

Mickey has enjoyed art ever since she was in elementary school. She has a small collection of oil-based paintings for sale at the gallery. Her favorite is hanging on the wall next to the cash register for the asking price of $3,000. Mickey wants to use the profits from the sale to pay for a missionary trip to Africa for two; herself and one other person, although at this time she does not know who that particular person will be. Connie is confident that it will sell, but Mickey is not convinced. Mickey stayed with her aunt for two weeks last summer and was inspired after one of her evening workouts on the beach. A large opening, developed in the clouds and sunrays burst onto the beach an illuminated the windows of the century-old Lakeshore Community Church. Connie refers to these occurrences as "Jesus clouds." The freshly painted white church, which appeared to have fire in the windows, inspired the young artist, and she spent the rest of that summer putting the image onto canvas. Mickey has also made one hundred limited edition prints of her painting and has them for sale at the gallery for $150 each. The couple from Chicago bought one of the limited edition prints and a 24" x 36" framed photograph of Aunt Connie's popular "Psalm 113:3" photograph. Connie is only taking 10% of the proceeds from Mickey's sales so the young artist has already commissioned well over $100 in her first hour of working at the gallery. Mickey's tanned features help make her beautiful smile all that much brighter. The young artist can't hide her obvious joy.

Tourists file in throughout the morning and the ladies sell three more photographs. Christian music flows from the speakers of an old stereo. In between customers, Mickey keeps busy making jewelry. She has decided that she is going to make anklets, bracelets and necklaces to sell in addition to her canvas oil prints. That morning Mickey has made a matching necklace and bracelet out of blue gems. If this morning is any indication of what the rest of the summer is going to be like, then this is going to be one epic summer. When the *Michael W. Smith* song *"You Won't Let Go"* comes on the radio, Connie sees that no one is in the store and cranks up the volume. The ladies happily sing right along, *"You are the anchor for my soul, You won't let go, You won't let go."*

At noon, the ladies begin to eat their homemade lunches; egg salad sandwiches, water melon slices and yogurt. While they are eating, a nurse, Donna Roberts, stops in to say "hi."

"Hi Donna, hey, what happened earlier? Two fire trucks and an ambulance went by the store this morning."

Donna shakes her head and responds, "A meth lab exploded a couple miles out of town. It killed the man who was attempting to make the drug. Unfortunately, the explosion badly injured a mother and her child who were residing in the house next door. I don't know if you two are aware, but southwest Michigan currently leads the country in meth addictions. It is a serious problem, and some would even describe it as an epidemic. Users have told me that their first experience with meth is the ultimate high. After that, they are simply *chasing the high*. They can never again satisfy that craving."

Instantly Mickey's eyes began to water and Aunt Connie quietly asks, "How bad are the woman and child injured?"

Donna replies, "I don't know the extent of their injuries, but they're both in critical care."

Mickey dabs at the tears in her eyes, and Aunt Connie bites her lip in anger. Both ladies quietly whisper silent prayers asking God for his healing touch.

Chapter 4

Josie Jones empties her hands by dropping her volleyball and water bottle on a towel. Knowing full well that she is being watched by the boys on the adjoining court, she casually slips off her faded blue jean shorts and pulls her t-shirt slowly up over her head. Donned in a fire engine red bikini that naturally highlights her deep brown skin tone, Josie is the very definition of a beach beauty. Pulling her long dark hair back to slip on a hair tie, Josie's eyes scan the parking lot for her partner. When she doesn't see her, she puts on a pair of mirrored Oakley sunglasses so that she can watch the boys watching her without them knowing that she is looking. Even though it is extremely vain, she craves the attention of others.

Mickey has ridden her bike back to the cottage, changed clothes and is now driving to North Beach in her new Jeep Wrangler. She just bought it the week before and knows it will be the perfect summer vehicle. Its rugged, sporty reputation matches her wild spirit.

Making the turn onto Dyckman Avenue, Mickey has to come to a full stop. Vehicles are lined up for the Bascule Drawbridge that is starting to rise so that tall boats can safely navigate the Black River. While waiting, she places her hair into a ponytail and finds her Oakleys in the glove compartment. Mickey passes time by singing along to the radio.

Mickey is anxious to meet up with Josie. They have been friends ever since her family started visiting South Haven. Josie grew up in this small town and developed into a very good volleyball player. Her parents divorced a few years back, and Josie lives with her mom. Her mom has to work two jobs to make ends meet, and Josie seldom sees her. Her dad moved to South Bend, Indiana, with his new girlfriend. She is closer to Josie's age then she is to his. Dad has been pretty much non-existent since the split. Loneliness is a common companion for this small town girl.

South Haven summers are fantastic, but the day after Labor Day, is when the tourists stop coming, and the weather quickly turns cold. Winters are brutal as lake effect snows dump huge amounts of the white powder on the somewhat empty streets. The strong western winds increase the chill factor to an unbearable level.

Volleyball provides an escape for Josie and has given her an identity. Josie received a sports scholarship to Western Michigan University, and she plays against Mickey's team at least once a year at the collegiate level. The two opponents are teaming up this summer to compete in a variety of Lake Michigan beach tournaments. The first tournament is held in South Haven during the Harbor Festival. This three-day event jump starts the summer season. It also includes musical entertainment and Dragon Boat racing, a team paddling sport that originated in ancient China.

When Mickey pulls into the North Beach parking lot, she sees a lone parking spot near the volleyball nets. She barely remembers to slip the jeep into park before bursting out the side and running straight into the arms of her awaiting friend. The boys are beaming from ear to ear. Now there are two hot girls to look at.

When the girls break their embrace, Mickey enthusiastically exclaims, "I've missed you!"

Josie smiles and returns the sentiment, "Me too."

Josie then bends down and picks up her volleyball. She starts backpedaling in the sand and shouts out, "Come on, let's warm up!"

The boys who were admiring the girls' physical beauty are now observing their obvious talent which far exceeds any other girls they have seen play. Two seventeen year old males challenge the girls to a game. Josie smiles smugly and states, "We'll give you a game to 21 if all four of you play. Two of you won't be enough competition."

Two blond-haired boys hear the dare and gladly jump at the opportunity to mingle with these hot girls. Josie throws the ball under the net and says, "You guys serve first. Make sure you pick a good server because you won't get a second opportunity!"

Josie is getting her swag on and Mickey, who doesn't talk smack, enjoys watching her crazy friend have fun at the younger guys' expense. When the shortest guy on the team serves the ball over the net, he accurately hits it to Mickey. Mickey makes a perfect pass to Josie who sets it precisely were Mickey wants it. Mickey spikes the ball off of the foot of the boy who served it. One zero, game on!

Josie takes the ball and immediately serves seven consecutive aces. On her eighth serve, the boys finally return the ball only to have Mickey set Josie who spikes the ball off of the arms and into the face of one of the opposing players. The boys are too young and dumb to be embarrassed. They're just glad to have the opportunity to play with these amazing girls. On Josie's next serve, she sails one long to give the boys their only point. The girls handle the incoming serve with ease and then Mickey makes good on her next seven serves for a 15-1 lead. They play on for an easy victory.

The boys prove to be good sports and shake the girls' hands before sheepishly departing. Josie had walked to the beach, so Mickey offers her friend a ride back to Connie's house for a free meal. Josie gladly accepts the invitation. While walking to the jeep, Josie glances back over her shoulder and is not disappointed. The boys are watching them walk away.

Chapter 5

Jack and Jerrid have a good first morning out on the lake. Their clients have caught their limit of fish and are happy. Jack is steering the thirty-one foot Tiara under the raised bridge when he sees a beautiful blond in a bright red drop-top Jeep. The four clients are still re-living their successful day of fishing and their conversation fades out as Jack stares in the direction of the jeep. He can see the girl singing along to her radio. It is obvious to him that she doesn't care who is watching; she is at peace with the world. Jerrid sees that Jack is distracted and looks in the direction of where Jack's eyes are glued. He should have known. Jack has already found the prettiest blond in town. Jerrid snaps his fingers in front of Jack's face and says, "Pay attention, I don't need you crashing this boat on our inaugural trip."

Jack nods, but the damage is done. The image of the girl in the jeep is ingrained into his brain. The game plan going into the summer was to get with as many girls as possible, but Jack knew in his heart that was only a fantasy. He has always been a one woman man, and he may have just seen the one for him. He hopes that she isn't just a day visitor like so many people who travel to South Haven. Hopefully she is one of the ones who will be spending the summer here. Time will tell. He must focus on completing his duties and sending the clients on their merry way with fresh fillets and a strong desire to return.

An hour later, the clients have had their photographs taken with their impressive catch as well as posed for pictures with the two famous athletes. They depart with large slabs of filleted fish and have a great story to tell their cronies when they arrive home. Jerrid cleans the fish cooler and Jack writes the daily logs which consist of actual time on the water, fuel use, what depth and water temperature were the fish biting, etc. Jack's mind is still clouded with the image of the beautiful blond he saw in the jeep.

As the men finish their task, another boat enters the slip next to them. Rap music fills the air and the passengers are loud and boisterous. A group of twelve swimsuit clad people are still partying after what looks like a fun filled day out on the Great Lake. Most of them are quite tanned and others sport sunburned skin. They will obviously feel the effect much worse once their alcohol wears off, but by the sound of the party, that may not occur for quite a while.

Leading the group of partiers is a tall muscular man with long curly hair. He looks like a California surfer. "Hey Rowdy, grab me another beer," yells out another guy who doesn't appear like he needs another one. The dude is stumbling and eventually falls while trying to step out onto the deck. The partiers laugh at the sun burned drunk as he struggles to upright himself into a sitting position on the decking. Blood starts to seep out of his fresh wounds, but no one bothers to help.

Rowdy jumps onto to the deck, steps over his fallen comrade and walks over to the charter boat. "Thayer, Stone, what are you two doing here?"

Jack and Jerrid look at the long-haired man, and it takes them each a second or two before they recognize him. It's Rob Bailey, the back-up point guard on the U of M basketball team. Neither of the guys have ever spoken with him but they have seen him on campus occasionally in the rec center. Rob is a superb athlete with amazing quickness. He also has a deadly long range jump shot. Word has it that he has the talent to start but carries such a poor attitude that he constantly finds himself in the coach's doghouse. Rob is very energetic and an adrenaline junkie. The Rowdy moniker seems to fit him well.

Jerrid replies, "We're running fishing charters for Mr. Garrison. What are you doing here?"

Rob runs his tanned fingers through his hair and exclaims, "I'm here for the party. My dad bought a summer house on the lake, and he's busy doing business in Europe so I am the caretaker while he is away. We're heading there now for some pizza and beer. If you guys are done, you ought to join us. A bunch of girls are supposed to meet us there."

Jerrid grins at Jack and then looks back at Rob and shouts out, "We're in!"

Chapter 6

Jack follows Rob's instructions to a big two-story home that has cedar shingle siding. The estate would easily fetch a million dollars at the current market rate. Jack drove his black drop-top jeep and the lake air feels refreshing after a long day in the sun. Before they walk the lighted steps to the pool area, the two athletes reapply deodorant and pull on fresh t-shirts. Their biceps bulge tightly at the sleeves. Jack scans the parking area for the bright red jeep but does not find it.

Loud music mixed with the sound of splashing water comes from the pool area. The party is rocking. When Jack and Jerrid walk through the cast iron gate, heads turn and a small group of girls are caught gawking at them. The attention is flattering.

Rob waves the guys over to the bar. Pizza boxes fill the counter space. They are very hungry and grab large slices of pepperoni pizza. Rowdy pops the top on two beers and thrusts them in front of them and asks, "So, what do think?"

Jerrid smirks and blurts out, "I think that this summer is off to a great start."

Jerrid takes a large bite and then asks, "So Rob, why do they call you Rowdy?"

Rob gets a crazed look on his face and replies, "Probably for doing stuff like this!"

With that being said, Rob climbs up onto the bar, jumps up and catches the edge of the roof with his hands. The muscular partier performs a flawless pull-up and then pushes himself up onto the roof. The partiers take notice of the stunt and start chanting, "Go Rowdy Go, Go Rowdy Go!"

Rob climbs to a high point of twenty-five feet and the chant changes to, "Jump, Jump, Jump!"

Rob jumps out, tucks his chin and performs a perfect flip before imperfectly entering the water on his backside when his body starts to rotate for a second time. The pool side crowd cheers for their crazy host as he emerges from the water. Once again the chants shout out; "Rowdy, Rowdy, Rowdy!"

Rob punches his fist into the air and lets out a loud yell. As he walks to the steps he high-fives people in the shallow end. Eventually he returns back to his new friends and asks, "Does that answer your question?"

Jerrid drains his beer and replies, "I would say that it does."

Jerrid then grabs Jack's beer and takes a large slug from it. He looks at Rowdy and says, "Jack doesn't drink, but I won't let his beer go to waste."

Rowdy's back is beet red from smacking the water but he does not feel any pain due to the large amount of alcohol he has consumed. Jack wonders if Rob is using more than just alcohol but he keeps this thought to himself.

As if on cue, three beautiful ladies walk up to the athletes and confidently introduce themselves. Frivolous small talk develops between them and Rob maintains a steady dialog which keeps the focus on him. Rob is in mid-sentence talking about himself when he is interrupted by a cry for help.

A young girl has passed out in the shallow end and is floating face down in the pool. A big guy with a wild looking chest tattoo lifts the girl from the water and carries her to the side of the pool. He lays her lifeless body flat on the cement and checks for a pulse. A friend of the girl states that she saw her do a line of cocaine about a half hour earlier. Hearing this, Jack and Jerrid exchange glances and start moving towards the parking lot. Coach would kill them if they were caught up in any news regarding drugs.

Jerrid glances over his shoulder at the pretty girls. Rob has not made a very good impression on Jack. He doesn't like to judge anyone too soon, but there are definitely red flags. Paradise sure is proving to have its share of problems.

Chapter 7

The following morning, while driving his Jeep to the boat docks, Jack observes a beautiful blond running on the beach. His head swivels and his eyes open wide. Jerrid turns to see what Jack is looking at and declares, "It's the same girl, Jack. That is your girl from yesterday."

Mickey runs much earlier on Tuesdays because she volunteers at the hospital. She is a pre-med major and has aspirations of becoming a doctor. Mickey's compassionate heart is compatible with a career in medicine.

Jack and Jerrid have charter clients waiting on them so they have to keep driving. Jack's mind is now clouded with thoughts of the pretty girl for whom he has yet to meet.

Later that morning, Mickey goes to the hospital dressed in her volunteer scrubs. She enters the nursing area and finds them engaged in a conversation about a young girl who was brought in during the night shift. Apparently, the teenager had overdosed on cocaine. Unfortunately, in this day and age that in itself is not shocking; but what has caused a big stir is the fact that it is Reverend Newhouse's youngest daughter, Stephanie. The charge nurse, Linda, is very concerned. She is close to the family. Stephanie just finished her junior year at South Haven High.

As the ladies are talking, a doctor comes around the corner and motions for Linda to come to him. He tells her that Stephanie will be ok and asks her to break the news to the Reverend and his wife who are currently praying in the hospital chapel. Linda looks very relieved and mouths, "Thank you, Jesus."

When Linda returns, she attends to her volunteer for the day. Linda gives Mickey her first assignment which is to assist a patient named Mary. Mary was brought in after her house caught fire. She is the lady who lived next to the meth lab explosion. Mary suffered smoke inhalation and a concussion from hitting her head when the explosion threw her into the wall. Mary's daughter was also admitted, but she was released yesterday and is staying with Mary's sister while her mother recovers.

Mickey enters the room and Mary is looking out the window with visible tears in her eyes. Mickey introduces herself and asks if she needs anything. Mary shakes her head "no," but Mickey knows that some people are naturally shy or don't like to ask for anything, so she presses on and asks, "Have you had breakfast yet?"

Mary sits up in her bed and quietly replies, "No."

Mickey smiles and says, "Well what would you like, how about eggs, toast and orange juice?"

Mary looks into Mickey's eyes and for the first time since she has been hospitalized she smiles, and kindly replies, 'Yes, I would like that."

Mickey says, 'Well then, I'll go get you some, but first let me open the window curtain all the way so that you can enjoy our South Haven sunshine!"

At 10 a.m. the doctor makes his rounds and approves Mary for discharge. Mary showers and gets dressed into a fresh set of clothes. Mickey returns with a wheelchair and tells Mary, "Everyone gets a free wheel chair ride to the front door."

Mary accepts, and Mickey wheels her outside. The first person to meet them is Mary's little girl. The single mother has a tearful reunion with her one and only daughter. Mickey hugs them both.

Before leaving for the day, Mickey visits Stephanie and shares a brief conversation with the saddened teenager. Mickey holds her hand as the young girl cries tears of guilt and shame. She tells Mickey, "I feel so stupid. I caved into peer pressure, and now I am so embarrassed. I've had a crush on this guy for a long time, and he finally showed an interest in me. He took me to the party and we weren't there very long before he started putting lines of cocaine on a mirror. He snorted a line and told me to do the same. I was so afraid of him not liking me that I did what he said before I even thought about the consequences."

Stephanie's tears quickly turned into sobs. Mickey holds her hand until she gets herself back under control. Mickey asks her if she can pray for her. Stephanie continues to cry but nods her head "yes."

Mickey prays, "Father in heaven, one of your special children needs you. She loves you and knows that she made a mistake. Please embrace her in your loving spirit and remind her how precious she truly is. Please give her strength to weather this storm and make it, a temporary mistake in her journey called life. In Jesus name we pray, Amen."

Stephanie squeezes Mickey's hand, looks her in the eye and quietly whispers, "Thank you."

Unknown to Mickey, God's grace, combined with Mickey's sincere kindness, strengthens the once vulnerable teenager. The transformation has already begun!

Chapter 8

Day two on the charter boat proves to be a good time. Four police officers, all in their mid-forties, are aboard and this spirited crew likes to have fun. Their main hobby is to unleash insults at each other much the same way athletes do in the security of the locker room. One heavyset man with a large belly is unmercifully called *Slim*. A Lieutenant who is having hair loss issues and doesn't want to give up the "flowing locks" maintains a comb over that does not fare so well while out to sea. At one point the Lieutenant attempts to make fun of Slim but the heavyweight quickly retorts, "Now don't make me *comb over* there and kick your butt!" This draws laughter from everyone on board except for the Lieutenant.

Jack and Jerrid are not immune from the verbal assault of cop humor and they are quickly nicknamed *Suspect One* and *Suspect Two*. The boys give as good as they take and voice concerns about becoming sick with the *swine flu*. The good nature ribbings quickly bond the jocks and cops.

The officers enjoy a fun-filled day of laughing and fishing. They successfully catch their limit and are in a great mood.

On the ride back to land the men are tired after a full day in the sun, and they start to relax and engage in shop talk. War stories circulate about the meth issues that are currently prevalent in rural southwestern Michigan. The addictive drug is labeled the "poor man's cocaine." It is cheap to make and very popular with rural America. Jerrid tells the officers about the house exploding. The officers nod their heads and tell their own stories of horror that they have encountered with meth labs.

They also speak of drug trafficking from Chicago up the Lake Michigan coast into Benton Harbor, South Haven and Saugatuck. Heroin is on the rise and Benton Harbor has had two recent deaths from "bad H" that has come out of Chicago. Two of the officers are on a drug task force unit that seized a semi-truck loaded with bales of marijuana on Interstate-94 just north of the Indiana state line.

Since the men have hit it off so well, Slim invites the boys to have a drink with them at one of the local watering holes. Jack and Jerrid agree to meet up with the policemen at the Jolly Roger, a bar and grill that looks out over the lake.

The bar provides a festive atmosphere with big screen televisions visible from every seat. Most of the TV's are turned to Detroit Tiger baseball. Slim orders two platters of appetizer consisting of hot wings, cheese sticks and jalapeno poppers. Jack and Jerrid happily indulge in the platter of food. Even though Jerrid is craving a beer he joins Jack and drinks a big glass of water while the older gents empty a couple pitchers of the alcoholic beverage. When Jack finishes his glass he sets it on the table and looks outside. His eyes nearly pop out of his head when the blond from the red jeep walks by accompanied by a pretty brunette.

Slim notices the spark in Jack's eyes and states, "One of them sure got your attention. Go ahead, you boys take off and have a good time."

Jack and Jerrid shake hands with their new friends and promptly leave in search of the two girls. The boys go out the door and onto the deck when they notice the red jeep leaving the parking lot.

A man carrying a guitar sees the boys and knows what's on their minds. He speaks up, "Do you want to know where they are going?"

Jack looks at the man and says, "Definitely!"

The guitarist tells them, "More than likely they are headed to North Beach. They play volleyball, and I would bet good money that is where they are going now."

Jack and Jerrid thank the man and then jump into Jack's jeep for the short ride to the beach.

Chapter 9

Jack punches the accelerator and burns a trail out of the parking lot. A few minutes later he can see the red jeep. Three cars separate them from the girls. Jerrid is pounding the dash raring to go. "Come on Jack, catch them. My grandma drives faster than this!"

Jack stomps on the accelerator and the jeep lurches forward. When he turns on to Dyckman Avenue he sees that the red jeep is the last vehicle allowed over the bridge. The stop light is red signaling that the bridge is going to be lifted, and the gates come down right behind the departing red machine. Denied! The boys are forced to wait. The delay adds to the suspense of the chase.

Fifteen minutes later, the black jeep enters the North Beach parking lot. Mickey and Josie are on the first court passing the volleyball back and forth. They look stunning. Their tanned athletic bodies radiate in the summer sun. The ladies, volleyball skills are flawless, and they make the exercise look elementary.

The four teenage boys from the other day are about to ask the girls for a rematch when they see Jack and Jerrid approaching the court. Jerrid gives the boys a, *don't even think about it* glare. Josie notices the interaction and is instantly attracted to the powerfully built and apparently quite confident, Jerrid.

Jack takes the lead and introduces himself to the girls, but it is obvious that his attention is directed at Mickey. Next he introduces his partner. Josie gives Jerrid a mischievous smile and introduces herself and Mickey to the two of them.

Not missing a beat, Jack proposes a game. He then proceeds to suggest that he and Mickey take on Jerrid and Josie. Both girls shake their heads "no" and Jack looks confused. Mickey ends the awkward moment by informing Jack, "Josie and I are a team; we will play against the two of you."

Before Jack can object, Josie blurts out, "Game to 21, must win by two, loser buys ice cream!"

Jerrid peels off his t-shirt and teases, "I hate to spend your money after just meeting you, but if you insist, I'll take an extra-large banana split!"

Josie notices a cool tribal tattoo on Jerrid's bicep and is intrigued. She throws the ball to the boys and tells them that they get to serve first. She then huddles up with her teammate. Mickey looks across the net and asks Josie, "Did you see their shirts? They were both wearing U of M shirts. We definitely have to beat them!"

Josie laughs and says, "They're not wearing any shirts now and I'll tell you what I noticed, their tight abs and bulging biceps. These guys are hot!"

Always the competitor, Mickey looks Josie in the eye and demands, "You can flirt with them after the game, right now let's beat them. Show no mercy!"

Jack casually tosses the ball in the air as he waits for the girls to get lined up for his serve. Jack has played a little bit of volleyball and foresees a quick victory. He is already picturing Mickey at the ice cream parlor.

The girls get into position, and Jack takes it easy and lobs a serve over to the one that he has eyes for. Mickey passes the ball to Josie who in turn sets the ball perfectly at the net. Mickey leaps high into the air and spikes the ball at the feet of the unsuspecting Jack.

Jack looks over at Jerrid and both men have a surprised expression on their faces. It looks like they've got a game on their hands. Their competitive juices start to flow.

Josie fires a serve at Jerrid and the ball hits off of his upper arm and ricochets out of bounds. Now both men have been schooled and it is 2 – 0 in favor of the girls. Josie's next serve splits the two men and the ace makes it 3 – 0. Her next serve is fired at Jack. He manages to pop it into the air. Jerrid hits it deep into the opposing side of the court and Josie passes it to Mick. Mickey sets up her teammate, but Josie's spike lands about an inch out of bounds for the boy's first point.

Twenty-five minutes later, the girls lead 20 – 11. Its Mickey's turn to serve and she shows no mercy. She gives the ball top spin so that it will dip as soon as it passes over the net. Both Jack and Jerrid dive for the short jump serve and end up with nothing but sand in their faces. The two Big Ten football players have just been spanked in an competitive event by a couple of girls.

They sheepishly get up and dust the sand off of their sweaty torsos. The girls are at the net smirking with their hands stuck out. The guys shake their hands and the girls tell them, "Good game."

The ice cream parlor is only a few steps away from the volleyball courts and the girls each get vanilla ice cream cones dipped in chocolate while both boys get banana split sundaes. Small talk develops and Mickey asks Jack, "Why are you both wearing U of M shirts?"

Jack proudly informs her, "We play football there. I am the starting quarterback and Jerrid is the starting inside Linebacker. Are you a U of M fan?"

Mickey vigorously shakes her head no and says with as much distain as she can muster, "No, I prefer *thee* University of Michigan, which of course is Michigan State University."

"Do you want me to believe that you prefer Moo U over the maize and blue?" Asks Jack in mock astonishment.

Mickey enjoys the playful banter and keeps it going by responding, "Well, I would find it very hard to cheer against myself since I play volleyball for the wonderful Green and White!"

Josie interrupts the steady dialog with her own college endorsement, "The Big 10 is over-rated; if you all want to pick a winner, root for the Western Michigan University Broncos. We will easily win the MAC title in volleyball because we have a pretty awesome brunette leading the team, and I personally know that she doesn't take any prisoners!"

The U of M football team is expected to compete for the national championship title as is the Michigan State volleyball team. The WMU volleyball team is projected to win their conference championship.

How cool is that? All four individuals are Division One athletes. Common denominators perk interest beyond the obvious physical attractions. There is no question about the match ups. Jack obviously has eyes for Mickey, and Jerrid and Josie seem to have hit it off as well.

The girls have to leave but give the boys their phone numbers after being asked. Josie can't help herself and teases Jerrid that she doesn't usually date losers and holds her fingers in the shape of an 'L' up to her forehead. Jerrid appreciates her sassiness and smirks.

In the parking lot, Jack compliments Mickey's ride, "Nice jeep."

Mickey smiles and says, "Yes, another common denominator." Then she teases, "Maybe it's a sign!" With that she puts the jeep into gear and rolls on out of sight.

Chapter 10

Aunt Connie notices that Mickey's mind is obviously elsewhere. She is texting way more than usual. No jewelry is being made on this day. At lunch Connie asks Mick, "What's up?"

Mickey blushes and tells her aunt that she has met a guy and that he asked for her phone number. Connie asks, "Where did you meet him, and more importantly, who is he?"

Mickey spends the next half hour rambling on about the volleyball game and Jack. Of course, the competitor includes the fact that she and Josie won the game. Her competitive drive is still firmly in place despite the strong feelings that she is developing for the Michigan quarterback.

Jack calls her a little after noon and asks her out on a date. Mickey accepts on the condition that it is a double-date with Josie and Jerrid. Jack agrees and makes plans for the foursome to have dinner the following night at The Fish Shack.

Mickey continues texting Josie late into the afternoon. They spend a large amount of time discussing what they will wear. They each conclude that they will wear capri pants, sleeveless tops and flip flops. Of course, Mickey will be accessorized with her home-made jewelry.

Jack and Jerrid have the afternoon off and decide to ride their mountain bikes across town to the outdoor basketball courts to shoot some hoops. They have to wear shirts while on the job so this gives them the opportunity for tanning while working out.

Two South Haven High School kids are already playing one-on-one when Thayer and Stone ride up. Jerrid gets off of his bike and asks the kid with the ball if he and Jack can join in. The kid looks at Jack and asks, "Are you Jack Thayer?"

Jack nods his head "Yes."

The kid looks star struck and stutters out a reply, "Well yeah, for sure, I mean…Yeah."

Jerrid looks at Jack and says out loud, "What am I, chopped liver?"

Jack smiles and introduces Michigan's starting linebacker, Jerrid Stone. This gesture seems to pacify Jerrid's ego.

The kid passes the ball to the Michigan quarterback and Jack takes a shot out past the 3-point circle and catches nothing but net. The other youngster passes the ball to Jerrid and he promptly does the same. While the four guys take turns shooting, a shiny black Chevy Silverado with a high lift-kit rolls up to the court, bumping loud rap music. The obnoxious bass vibrates the windows and thumps the inner ears of everyone around.

Rowdy Rob jumps out of the driver's seat with three of his buddies in tow. Rob struts onto the court and immediately starts to talk some smack. "Are you two lost? This is a basketball court. Shouldn't you two be elsewhere?"

Jack takes the bait and replies, "We didn't think that this game could be all that difficult since our school offers it as a *girls* sport!"

Jack actually meant his statement to be good-natured ribbing, but thin-skinned Rob takes offense to the comment and is determined to make Jack pay. Rob's demeanor changes, and he suggests a game of four on four; him and his friends against the four of them. Jack doesn't think that the teams are fair considering that the two guys that are teamed with him and Jerrid are only fifteen, but his competitive nature is up for the challenge.

On the very first possession Rob utilizes a screen from one of his teammates and drives to the hole for the first basket of the game. Jack brings the ball up the court and finds Jerrid open after he filters through the lane. Jack hits Jerrid with a powerfully quick pass and Jerrid ties the game one, one.

As the game progresses, it becomes obvious that Rob's game plan is for him to score all of the points. He takes all of the shots and yells at his teammates to set screens for him. Rob's team is leading ten to eight when Jack rebounds a missed three-point attempt that Rob has shot. Jack takes off on a fast break with only Rob on the defensive end. Jack's competitive juices flow and he steps just inside the free throw lane and leaps high into the air. Rob tries to block the shot, but Jack is much too powerful and throws down a thunderous dunk. Everyone gasps and then howls at the unbelievable play. One of the high school kids yells out. "Postered!"

Jack jogs down to the opposite end of the court while everyone is chattering about his impressive play. The damage is done. Rob is embarrassed. Even though Rob makes every one of his next few shots to win the game, his ego is badly bruised. He now carries a vengeance for Jack: Somehow, some way, he will get back at him.

Chapter 11

Jack and Jerrid arrive right on time for their date. They meet up with the girls at Connie's cottage. After a proper introduction to Aunt Connie, they get in the black jeep for the short ride to the restaurant. They are all in excellent shape, tanned and feeling quite confident. If the jeep carried an energy meter it would be buried in the red due to the amped-up excitement level.

The restaurant host seats them at a table on the outside deck. The same guy who was playing guitar at the Jolly Roger is serenading the diners with various Bob Seger and Jimmy Buffet songs. Michiganders absolutely love Bob Seger. As the girls are being seated, the guitarist gives the boys the thumbs up sign. Jack and Jerrid acknowledge the gesture with big smiles and the casual nodding of their heads.

Both girls order perch dinners and the boys order fish platters which include walleye, perch and skewered shrimp. Josie is an instigator and brings up the volleyball game. "Maybe you guys should recruit a third or fourth player to give your team a fighting chance against us."

Jerrid shakes his head and responds, "I didn't think that you would have dinner with us if we beat you... so we let you win."

Without missing a beat Josey retorts, "Was the sand sandwich you ate on the last serve part of the ploy also?"

Jack looks over at Jerrid and says, "She has us on that one. You girls are good. Are you playing in any of the summer tournaments?"

Mickey proudly exclaims, "You bet. We are teaming up and competing in the upcoming Harbor Festival Tournament."

The dinner banter continues and the collective personalities quickly blend. On a scale of one to ten, this first date would be an eleven!

After dinner the foursome go to South Beach and walk the pier out to the lighthouse. A steady parade of boats enter the mouth of the Black River between the two piers. Rowdy's boat enters the river and as it was the last time, it is loaded with passengers who themselves look loaded. Rowdy sees Jack and Jerrid and yells out to them, "Wolverines!" The other partiers on the boat join in and do their own chorus of shouts, "Wolverines!" Jack and Jerrid politely wave to the boaters. Next thing you know, Rowdy has dropped his trousers and is shining the moon. Laughter erupts among the boat passengers.

Jack is amused and embarrassed at the same time. He tells the girls that Rowdy is on the Wolverine basketball team and that he is staying in South Haven for the summer. A red haired guy with a matching red sunburn attempts to throw a can of beer to them, but it falls way short and smashes into the boulders lining the pier. The partiers on the boat laugh and call him names. The boat slowly exits their presence and Mickey is glad. She doesn't particularly like the party scene. Nothing good ever comes out of being drunk.

At the end of the pier, a couple of teenagers are fishing. Jack and Jerrid engage them in some fisherman dialog. Neither of the teens has had any luck on this particular night, but the youngest boy tells them about a good sized trout that he caught the night before. His eyes pop with excitement as he retells his tale. It is readily apparent that both Jack and Jerrid have a deep passion for fishing. The girls notice the attention that the guys give to the younger boys and believe that it translates into men with good hearts.

The two couples pair up and watch the sun set on the horizon. Josie gets her phone out and starts taking pictures. She has Jack and Mickey pose with the setting sun behind them and then asks them to take a photo of her and Jerrid. Next she wants one of her and Mickey. Then Josie asks one of the teen fishermen to take a photograph of all four of them. What a great conclusion to an awesome night. As they walk back to the jeep, Jack takes a hold of Mickey's hand and Jerrid does the same with Josie. Mickey's mind races with many different thoughts. Where is this going? Will it last through the summer? She then tells herself, "Shut up and enjoy the moment!" The moonlight dances off the water and all is well. Maybe this place really is *South Heaven.*

Chapter 12

Thunder and lightning erupt in the skies over Lake Michigan. The storm will soon hit land. White-capped waves crash ashore with some of the bigger swells cresting five feet high. Nothing highlights God's ultimate power more than a lightning storm out over the Great Lake. The fury of an angry sea is best seen from land.

An elderly couple, Fred and Louanne Warden, have already called in and cancelled their fishing excursion for the day. Jack and Jerrid have been fairly busy and welcome a day of rest. Around noon they are tucked safely inside their summer home playing a game of Madden Football when the doorbell rings. Jerrid goes to the door and finds Rowdy holding a case of beer and a bag full of tacos from Taco Bell. Rowdy blurts out, "Do you know what's good about being a narcissist? Me."

Jerrid laughs out loud and welcomes in the beer-toting visitor. Jack doesn't drink beer, but he is famished and digs into the bag of tacos. Rowdy and Jerrid pop the top of their canned beers and put the rest in the fridge.

"I figured a rainy day would be a good day to hang with you two. How are you guys doing? Isn't South Haven amazing?" Rowdy asks questions without really expecting answers. He is quite content on doing the talking.

These boys spend the rest of the afternoon playing more Madden football and mix in an occasional game of pool. Thunder continues to rumble throughout the afternoon. Bad jokes are told and all in all a good time is had. Rowdy has a gregarious personality and he cracks

Jerrid up with his many tales of misadventure. Jerrid laughs hysterically; as Rowdy tells him about the time that he and some high school buddies released greased pigs in the mall. His imitations of the mall security guards chasing the greased piglets has him doubling over in laughter. Jack also laughs but he is more measured with his responses. He is hesitant to fully embrace Rowdy. Jack's sensors warn him that Rowdy's self-centeredness could be a concern. Jack learned a long time ago to rely on his gut feelings and intuition. Rowdy not only likes to party but he likes to be the life of the party. It's evident that he thrives on attention and needs a daily fix to survive.

Around three o'clock the rain stops. Rowdy looks at his phone and abruptly stands and says that he has to leave. He says that he has an appointment that he has to attend to. Due to the afternoon of heavy drinking, Jack suggests that he should drive Rowdy to his appointment, but his argument falls on deaf ears. Rowdy gets in his vehicle and abruptly leaves. As suddenly as he arrived, he is gone.

Jack comments, "I get a bad feeling from Rowdy. He's trouble and I don't trust him. I could easily see him turning on us if things don't go his way. He made that joke about being a narcissist but it's also true."

Blurry-eyed, Jerrid shakes his head and says, "He's harmless; he's just a partier looking for a good time. I, for one, have no problem with that." A few minutes later, Jerrid crashes on the coach into a deep sleep.

****

Mickey has to open and close the gallery by herself due to Aunt Connie volunteering with a blood drive at the high school. Connie volunteers for a lot of community events and is an excellent role model for her young niece. Mickey knew that there wouldn't be a lot of business on a rainy day so she decided to start an oil painting of the image from last night. Josie forwards the photographs from the pier, so Mickey is going to paint the lighthouse with the sun setting on the horizon out over the lake. Painting allows her to capture her memories.

Just before noon, an elderly couple, Fred and Louanne Warden, come into the gallery. Louanne browses and Fred takes up a position next to Mickey. He is fascinated with severe weather and bends her ear about the day's storm activity. One tidbit of information that perks Mickey's interest is the fact that there have actually been tsunamis on Lake Michigan. Fred tells her, "When a tsunami happens on a Great Lake it is called a *seiche*. On June 26, 1954, a ten foot high inland tidal wave hit Chicago and killed eight anglers who were fishing on a pier. My wife and I were supposed to go fishing today. We had a charter boat scheduled but we cancelled. I have way too much respect for stormy weather and I was not going to risk our lives out at sea on a day like this."

Mickey asks, "Which charter service were you going to use?"

"The Wolverine. Personally, I am a Michigan State grad so I had some apprehension about getting aboard that vessel anyway," boasts the elderly man.

Mickey smiles and proudly informs the man, "Well you came to the right place. I am a current Michigan State student and am filled with Spartan pride." Just hearing about the fishing charter makes Mickey think of Jack. As it is, he is never too far removed from her thoughts.

Louanne reappears at the sales counter after picking out a small eight by ten plaque that has Psalm 23 layered over one of Aunt Connie's photographs. Mickey takes this opportunity to show the couple a photograph that Connie took of a pair of water spouts. She actually got the spectacular image from her back deck. The elderly gentleman loves it and tells his wife to buy it. Mickey rings up the sale and looks forward to telling Connie about her interactions with Fred and matching his interest with an item in the store.

As the couple leaves the gallery, Fred looks back at Mickey and smiles, "Go Spartans!" As always, Mickey has made a new friend.

Mickey closes the gallery at 5 p.m. The rain had stopped a couple of hours ago but the skies are still overcast. At 6 p.m. she meets up with Josie at North Beach for their nightly volleyball session. By 6:30 the girls are doing some hitting, aiming their spikes at a ball bag strategically placed on the other side of the net. While they are performing this maneuver, Jack rides up on his mountain bike. The girls decide to take a water break and meet up with the welcomed intruder. Josie asks, "Where's Jerrid?"

Jack responds, "We had the day off of work and Rowdy stopped over with some beers. Let's just say Jerrid wasn't in any shape to go riding with me tonight."

Josie's a little disappointed that Jerrid didn't come with Jack, but her attention is quickly perked when she notices two older men walking the beach looking at her.

Mickey looks deeply into Jack's eyes and asks, "What about you? Did you drink?"

Jack shakes his head no and replies, "No, I don't drink."

"Why not?" asks Mickey.

Jack looks out over the lake and says, "It's a long story, I'll be glad to tell you Saturday if you go out on a second date with me."

Mickey attempts to act casual, but her heart is racing on the inside. She calmly looks at Jack and comments, "I have Saturday off; what are you thinking?"

Jack sheepishly smiles and says, "Common denominator!"

Mickey looks puzzled and before she can say anything Jack asks, "Can you be ready at 11 a.m.?"

Looking surprised that he asked for time so early in the day she gladly answers, "Yes."

Jack climbs aboard his bike and says, "Good I'll see you then." With that said the cavalier jock puts his muscular legs to work and rides away. Mickey can't see it, but there is a big smile covering his rugged suntanned face!

Chapter 13

Jack arrives at Connie's cottage precisely at 11 a.m., and his shiny black jeep has an orange flag waving high in the air. Mickey is quick to solve the puzzle. Common denominator was referring to the fact that both of them have jeep wranglers. A jeep with an orange flag attached to the rear bumper means a trip up the coast to the Silver Lake Sand Dunes. This State Park has off-road access to sand-dunes which are three miles long and one and a half miles wide. Mickey gives Jack credit. They share the *common* interest of wrangler jeeps and there is no place better for off-road riding. Mickey thinks to herself, "The boy has done well."

The sun smiles on them as they drive up the coastal highway. Jack steals a look at the beautiful girl riding shotgun, she sparkles when she smiles. Right now she is a happy gal, so her smile is readily evident. She puts on one of Jack's camouflage ball caps and places her pony tail through the back hole of the cap so that her hair doesn't whip into her face. She turns and asks, "Would you take me hunting?"

Jack gets a playful look and responds with a defiant "no."

Mickey is surprised to hear such a quick no. "Why not," she protests.

Jack smirks when he says, "Because I need to pay attention when I hunt and you would definitely be a distraction. Sorry, but you are just too cute!"

Mickey returns with a smirk of her own and then challenges, "You're just afraid that I would shoot a bigger buck than you. You're scared to be shown up by a girl."

At this point they both crack up at their own playful banter. Neither of them take themselves too seriously, so they are both able to joke at their own expense without causing any hurt feelings. Everything just feels right.

Kenny Chesney blasts through the speakers and Mickey starts singling along to *"Summertime"*. Seeing Mickey singing takes Jack back to the first time that he saw her singing in her jeep. Once again he appreciates how comfortable she is in her own skin. With no apprehension she is not afraid to just be herself.

Kenny and Mickey finish their duet. Jack enters the State Park and finds the nearest trailhead. The dunes are breathtakingly beautiful. It's a bluebird day with no clouds in the sky. Although the sun is hot, the cool air blowing off of the lake makes it an ideal day. Jack climbs the first hill that he sees and the Jeep Wrangler handles it with ease. Mickey is having a blast. She is fearless. Jack steals a glimpse of Mick every chance that he gets. She is absolutely gorgeous and appears to be in her element whenever the sun hits her skin.

About an hour into their adventure, Jack pulls over and tells Mickey that it's her turn to drive. Mickey shows no hesitation and jumps at the opportunity. She shows a lot of grit and Jack is attracted to her intense devotion to whatever she pursues. Mickey climbs the highest dune and temporarily shuts down the four wheel drive machine so that she and Jack can enjoy the magnificent view. Actor Tim Allen does voice-overs for a series of Michigan tourism commercials that all end with the catch phrase, "*Pure Michigan.*" This spot and moment in time reminds Mickey of these sentimental commercials. Life is good right now. Mickey takes her phone and captures a photo of her and Jack, king and queen of the mountain! They both approve of their picture. Mickey starts the jeep back up and races it down the hill towards the beach.

After a couple of hours of dune riding, the happy couple leave the park, turn south and head back toward South Haven. The music is turned off and the conversation turns somewhat serious as they attempt to delve deeper into who the other person really is. Mickey once again asks Jack, "So why don't you drink?"

Jack answers the question with a question, "Do you drink?"

Mickey crinkles her brow because Jack hasn't yet answered her question but answers "no."

Jack asks, "Why not?"

"I'll gladly tell you why not after you give me your answer."

Jack gets a serious look on his face and then speaks in a very deliberate manner. "I made a promise to my father that I would not drink alcohol, and I am a man of my word. Both of my grandfathers were alcoholics and died well before their time. My dad broke the chain of alcoholism and made me promise to do the same. I have personally seen the destruction that alcohol can cause. My dad's brother followed in his father's footsteps and killed a family of three when his car crossed the center-line while he was driving drunk. My uncle was given a ten year prison sentence for three counts of manslaughter, but he received a life sentence in guilt."

Mickey lets the heavy words sit in the air before responding. "That's very honorable Jack. Watching loved ones suffer is one of life's greatest curses. I also have a grandfather who is an alcoholic. If my mom wants to talk to him, she has to do it before noon because he is too drunk the rest of the day. It makes me sad when I see the hurt in my mother's eyes that she feels for her father. Many people our age act like there are no consequences for their behaviors or actions but we both know that there can be long-term effects."

"Is that why you don't drink?" ask Jack.

"Actually no, it goes much deeper than that. It is part of the reason but not the whole reason. I am a Christian, so I choose not to drink."

Jack looks a little confused and asks, "Jesus made water into wine. I know Christians who drink. They say that the Bible doesn't say that you can't drink it just says that you can't be drunk. Is that your take on it?

Mickey measures her words and then replies, "Yes, that is true, but the Bible also says in 1 John 3:7 'Dear children, do not let anyone lead you astray. The one who does what is right is righteous.' If I drink and it leads you to drink with your family history of alcoholism, then I would be responsible for leading you astray. That is not righteous. When I die and go to heaven, I want to hear Jesus say, 'Well done my good and faithful servant.'"

Jack has never been a religious person, but he can tell that Mickey actually lives what she believes. He is strongly drawn to her and to the strength that she projects. Mickey's inner beauty matches her outward physical beauty, and Jack knows that is a rare trait. He has often thought that Christians appear very hypocritical, but Mickey appears to be the real deal.

When Jack drops Mickey off at the cottage, he gets out and walks her to the front door. Mickey's smile continues to radiate, and Jack can't get enough of the dynamic girl. Mickey stops at the door and faces her handsome date. Without skipping a beat Mickey asks, "Will you go to church with me tomorrow? Service starts at eleven and I'd like you to have dinner with Connie and me afterwards."

Jack asks as if it really matters, "What's on the menu?"

Mickey responds, "Steak."

Jack nods his head and comments, "I look forward to it. I will be here tomorrow morning at 10:30."

Mickey enthusiastically hugs Jack, lifts her head and gives him a quick kiss on the lips. Just as suddenly, she turns and goes inside.

Chapter 14

Jerrid had called Josie on Friday morning and set up a date for Saturday evening. Jerrid told Josie about the Black River Covered Bridge a few miles from South Haven, located on the Kal-Haven trail. She replied that she wanted to see it. They decided to ride their mountain bikes out there and have a picnic dinner.

Jerrid brings fried chicken, potato chips and dip. Josie brings home-made brownies and bottled water. They carry the food in back packs. Jerrid thought out the events in advance and made a prior trip to the bridge and stashed a blanket and a cheap cooler filled with beer.

Josie looks fantastic in her spaghetti strapped tank top and khaki shorts. Jerrid rides behind her admiring her tanned legs. Jerrid and Josie share a mischievous disposition and enjoy teasing each other. Josie's free-spirit attitude is just what Jerrid has been looking for.

Josie yells out without looking behind her, "Hey football stud, are you looking at my butt?"

Jerrid elicits a nervous laugh as if he has just been busted and lets out an unconvincing "no."

Josie continues to tease by displaying shock horror, "Well you should be; it's fantastic!"

This comment completely catches Jerrid off guard and he counters with, "I am a weak man and YES, It is fantastic!"

Josie turns around and flashes Jerrid a smug grin. She is quite pleased to hear that Jerrid likes what he sees!

Josie finds the covered bridge to be highly romantic and asks Jerrid to take pictures of her as she does various poses on and around the bridge. Jerrid happily obliges.

Josie loves attention and has always had the need to be in the spotlight.

Jerrid leads Josie to a secluded area under a sprawling oak tree where he has stashed the cooler of beer and a blanket. Josie starts unpacking her pack when Jerrid surprises her with a cold beer. Josie momentarily hesitates because she knows that she doesn't always handle alcohol well, but she also sees this as a dare, and she is not one to pass up a dare. She takes a sip of the beer and then Jerrid pops the top of another one and drinks half of a can with one long drink.

The food taste good and the landscape is majestically serene. The only sounds that can be heard are the wind blowing through the trees and song birds chirping. The athletes exchange stories about their upcoming seasons and the expectations that exist. Jerrid can see the passion that Josie has for volleyball. She talks excitedly about being elected team captain. She has her sights firmly set on a conference championship, and being named MAC player of the year.

Jerrid drinks three beers while eating dinner and Josie finishes one. Jerrid gives Josie a second beer and gets himself a fourth. They casually talk about their summer activities. After finishing their beers they lay on the blanket listening to the song birds. A weird sound comes from a nearby woods and Jerrid asks Josie if she knows what that sound was. She does not. He tells her that it is a turkey gobbling and that male turkeys gobble to let the female turkeys know where they are. Josie teases, "You gobbled your dinner. Are you trying to let me know that you are here?"

Jerrid replies, "In the wild turkey world, the hen, which is the female, goes in search of the tom, which is the male. " Are you searching for the tom?"

Josie leans over closer to Jerrid and says, "I found you."

For the first time, Jerrid and Josie kiss. The beer has made Josie a little light-headed and the first kiss leads to another and another. Josie's fingers outline the tribal pattern of the tattoo on Jerrid's rights bicep and she asks, "Do you have any other tattoos?"

Jerrid smugly replies, "You'll have to find out for yourself. Do you have any tattoos?"

Josie grin's her mischievous grin and replies, "You'll find out soon enough."

Soon thereafter the teasing turns to pleasing. Jerrid now knows that Josie doesn't have any tattoos!

Chapter 15

Jack pulls into Connie's driveway precisely at 10:30 a.m. on a glorious Sunday morning. Connie and Mickey come outside to greet him wearing sun dresses and matching pearl necklaces. Mickey's hair is not ponytailed, nor wind-whipped; it rests softly on her shoulders. Jack has been attracted to Mickey since day one, but right now she looks utterly stunning! If there was ever an angel on earth, this is what one would look like. Wide-eyed Jack blurts out, "You look beautiful."

Connie dryly replies, "Thank you."

Jack looks startled and before he can say anything further, Connie and Mickey start laughing.

Jack is momentarily embarrassed, but is quickly over it when Mickey sincerely answers with her own, "Thank you."

The three of them walk down the street to the Lakeshore Community Church that Mickey so skillfully captured in her *Jesus Cloud* painting. Jack holds Mickey's hand. Connie leads them into the church where they are greeted by two smiling ushers. Connie then walks to the second wooden pew. Mickey and Jack take a seat, but Connie sets her Bible down and walks over to the piano. Connie is an accomplished pianist and provides background music as the congregation of two hundred people file in.

The service starts at eleven with lively music. Accompanying Connie is a drummer and the guitar man from the restaurants. Jack thinks to himself, "That guy sure gets around."

Jack steals another glimpse at Mickey. She definitely looks like she is in her element but then again she always appears to be at peace with herself. Jack just can't get enough of this girl.

The minister delivers a powerful message on ones purpose in life. His bullet points are formed around two questions. Why are we on planet earth and where are we going in the afterlife? These are two questions that Jack has not previously pondered. If there is truly a God, and Jack definitely believes that there is, then what does he expect of us, and what does one have to do to get to heaven in the afterlife? Jack has always been a man of his word and he attempts to do what's right. Is that enough or is there more? The service ends with everyone singing the hymn, *Farther Along.*

After the service, the congregation mingles and socializes. A pretty teenager walks up to Mickey and gives her a big hug. Tears start to appear in the younger girls eyes. After they embrace Mickey politely introduces Jack to Stephanie. Jack politely says, "It's nice to meet you."

Stephanie says, "It's nice to meet you as well."

Stephanie then turns back towards Mickey and expresses gratitude for her kindness and prayer at the hospital. Next she whispers into Mickey's ear, "That was my first time trying drugs and by the grace of God I am committed to never doing that again. Greater is He that is in me than he that is in the world."

Mickey returns with words of encouragement and Stephanie knowingly shakes her head in approval.

Jack is continually amazed at the positive impact that Mickey has on so many lives. The reverend makes a point of introducing himself to Jack, and just like his daughter, he expresses his sincere gratitude to Mickey for her compassion at the hospital towards his daughter.

When the church attendees exit the sanctuary, they are once again greeted with a bright sunny day. The walk back to Connie's is nice. Sailboats can be seen scattered out on the lake. In the past, Jack would have much preferred to be out on the lake rather than at a church service but now the thought of what a great service those people on the boats missed, enters his mind. Life is often ironic.

When they get to the cottage, Connie hits play on her iPod which is sitting on a Bose speaker deck. and Josh Garrels sings a much different version of the same hymn that was played at the end of the service. Josh's version of *Farther Along* is part folk and part rap but in both cases the words seep deeply into Jack's thought process. *"Farther along we'll know all about it, farther along we'll understand why. Cheer up my brother, live in the sunshine. We'll understand it all bye and bye."*

Connie and Mickey start preparing lunch. Mickey is cutting lettuce and vegetables for a garden salad and Connie is seasoning the steaks. Connie asks Jack to start the grill. Jack ignites the gas and volunteers to grill the steaks. Connie gladly takes him up on his offer.

Lunch is magnificent. The three of them eat out on the deck to the sound of the waves washing ashore. Connie asks Jack a fair amount of questions, but is careful not to embarrass her niece. Jack steers the conversation towards Mickey and her upcoming beach tournament. "Are you and Josie going to win?"

Mickey's competitive spirit is always apparent. She bites her lower lip and calmly moves her head up and down, signaling a definite "yes."

Jack looks into her eyes and has no doubt that she will win. The intensity in her eyes reveals the heart of a champion. He is familiar with the look. He has seen it many times over on the gridiron. More importantly, his opponents have seen it in him.

After lunch Mickey and Jack go for a swim in Lake Michigan. They have fun floating in the swells and enjoy the inland ocean which is unsalted and without sharks. Afterwards they sun themselves while relaxing in the beach chairs that they carried down to the waterfront.

Jack feels really fortunate to spend so much quality time with Mickey and is curious as to why she doesn't already have a boyfriend. In this relaxed atmosphere he chooses to ask her, "So how is it that you don't already have a boyfriend?"

Mickey sighs and replies, "I've been putting off this conversation, but it's a conversation that I must have with you. I had a boyfriend for over a year but he broke up with me when I wouldn't have sex with him. Like you, I am also someone who keeps their word and I made a commitment to God that I would not have sex until I am married. Does that mean that I don't have temptations? No, far from it, but I take my Christianity seriously. God makes it clear in his Word that sex should be saved for marriage. I want His very best for my life and I intend to live up to His commands."

An awkward silence hangs in the air and Jack is not sure how to reply. Mickey gets a lump in her throat and she is afraid that Jack will choose to move on. She really likes this guy and hopes that he will stay. The silence feels like an eternity.

Finally Jack speaks, "Mickey, I am not sure where this relationship will lead, but for now I am all in. You are the most beautiful girl that I have ever met and your inner beauty is as spectacular as your incredible outer beauty! I'll respect your wishes and I want to learn more about your God. Your integrity and passion for life is addictive. To be honest, I entered this summer thinking only of myself. I have never met anyone like you, and I am looking forward to spending the rest of the summer with you if not well beyond. I feel lucky that I am in your life."

Mickey's heart feels like it is going to bust through her chest and she silently whispers a prayer, "Thank you, Lord!"

Chapter 16

It's 7 a.m. when Mickey pulls into the North Beach parking lot. The breeze coming off the lake is rather cool, but the weather report is calling for a daytime high of 88 degrees. Mickey reports in at the Harbor Festival tournament registration table. Their first game is at 8 a.m. Mickey and Josie are expected to compete for the championship, but there are two teams of Penn State girls who will provide serious competition.

Mickey is stretching on court one when Josie arrives. Josie is looking rough. She appears rather pale and sluggish. Josie plops down in the sand and apologizes for being late. Looking very concerned, Mickey asks her partner if she is ok. Josie shakes her head and says, "Not really. I went out with Jerrid again last night and he likes to drink beer. I drank a few too and must have had a few too many because I woke up this morning puking. I am off to a rough start, but I'll be fine."

Josie takes a long pull on a Red Bull energy drink and then joins Mickey with pre-game stretching. Next they get up and pass the ball back and forth. Josie asks Mickey if she went out with Jack last night. Mickey answers, "Yes" and tells her about their night at the movies capped off with a visit to the Dairy Queen. Ice cream is her guilty pleasure.

It sounds boring to Josie but she thinks to herself, "To each their own." Josie's night consisted of beers and pizza at the Jolly Roger and then a two-person party at Jerrid's summer place, which included skinny dipping in the pool and a follow-up session in tribal tattoo man's bed. Jerrid is spontaneous and fun. He's also just enough of a bad boy to keep Josie's attention. Josie doesn't include these details in her conversation with Mickey because she knows that Mickey is a straight-laced Christian, and in all honesty, she sometimes feels guilty around her. Josie knows that she doesn't measure up to Mickey's high standards and at times she wishes that she did. Mickey regularly invites her to church, but her attendance is sporadic at best. Her main fear is that church will interfere with her fun, and she is too young to comply by society rules. In her mind, she is in her prime and wants to indulge in what feels good.

Josie is definitely "under the weather," but she is also too competitive to allow a night of partying to interfere with her play. When the girls work on some pre-game hitting, she feels her athletic strength emerging. Eight a.m.; game on!

Josie's play is a little erratic in game one. Mickey's skills emerge and they win the first game 21 – 16 against a team that is much weaker than they are. By game two, Josie performs like her typical self and they win 21-4.

The next match is at 10:15, and the two-some remain in the winner's bracket with two solid victories. The other team only scores a total of 15 points in the two games. Josie notices that most of the guys come over to their court and watch them while they are playing. She doesn't think that the boys are there to watch their volleyball skills.

Mickey and Josie meet up with the lesser of the two Penn State teams and beat them soundly. The championship game will be at 4 p.m. and they will be playing the other Penn State team that has two girls who are both over six feet tall.

Prior to their final game, the girls snack on turkey sandwiches and apple slices. Jack and Jerrid have finished their day of guiding on the Great Lake and have come to watch their girls play in the championship game. Mickey and Josie are quite pleased that the guys have made it and show them through affectionate hugs. A full day in the sun has made the girls look even better in the minds of their two main fans.

The first game proves to be a tough battle but the girls hold onto a 21 – 19 win. With the score tied 19 -19, Mickey dug deep into her well of inner-strength and served out for the victory. By game two Mickey and Josie are simply unstoppable and they easily win 21 – 11. The hometown girl and her former Michigan Miss Volleyball playing teammate stand victorious. After shaking the opposing team's hands the girls hug in celebration of their crowning achievement. Jack and Jerrid play football in front of a 100,000 adorning fans, but now the roles are reversed, and they are the ones standing on the sideline clapping in appreciation.

Chapter 17

Mickey, Jack, Josie and Jerrid decide to celebrate with a victory dinner at The Fish Shack. The girls are going to go to Connie's to clean up and the boys agree to pick them up at seven. When Jack arrives, the girls jump up into his jeep before he even has a chance to stop. The girls act rather giddy and the boys are quite amused. The ride to the restaurant is lively and all four of them sing along to Jake Owen's *Barefoot Blue Jean Night*. Both girls are rocking faded Levi's and wearing flip-flops. Of course, they also have matching anklets that Mickey made. Fun is on tonight's agenda.

Laughter is quite common with the four diners and the girls are still on a natural high reliving their moments of glory. Jack and Jerrid knowingly look on. They definitely understand the thrill of victory and let the girls go on with their spirited review of the day.

Rumors of a beach party have circulated throughout the day. Josie has found out that it is at the Rio estate. Mickey feels hesitant about attending because she knows that there will be drinking, but her sense of adventure allows her to go. After all, she feels safe when she is with Jack. No one in their right mind would want to tangle with either Jack or Jerrid. Naturally, Mickey has already noticed that most of the other guys give them a wide path.

The Rio family owns property that sits on one thousand feet of the Lake Michigan shoreline. One of their grandsons has invited virtually everyone in town between the ages of eighteen and twenty-eight. The lakeshore sits back quite away from the road. When Jack drives his black jeep down a two-track driveway, he sees that there are already quite a few cars and trucks parked in a mowed yard the size of a football field. The yard sits high on a bluff. Wood steps wind down to the beach about 200 feet below, but most of the party-goers run down a sandy slope. The two couples follow a group of girls down the hill and have a hearty laugh when Jerrid runs out into the lead and tumbles into a summersault after losing control. He gets to his feet laughing and lets everyone know that he is alright.

At the base of the hill, Josie jumps up onto Jerrid's back and Mickey does the same to Jack. The muscular men easily carry their light piggy-backers over to where a crowd is gathered around a massive bonfire. After another 80 degree day, everyone is quite tanned, and no one in this crowd has any self-esteem issues.

Once again the guitar man makes an appearance. He is everywhere. The guy is probably in his late twenties or early thirties and quite fit. Rumor has it that he is spending his summer in a houseboat docked at the marina and playing gigs for spending money. Apparently he just got out of the service, and after serving three tours overseas, he just wants to chill for the summer. The music man is quite talented. Ironically, he is singing *Barefoot Blue Jean Night*, the same song that the girls had sung earlier in the night.

There is a crowd of about seventy people milling around the fire, and everyone joins in when he sings the chorus. Jack glances at Mickey, and she has her arm around Josie. The two of them are swaying back and forth as they sing along to the catchy tune.

When the song finishes, Jerrid has already found the beer and has one in each hand. He offers one to Josie but she declines. Jerrid looks at her confused and Josie explains to him that she was sick this morning. After a long day in the sun, she knows that she won't be able to keep it down, so she has to decline. Jerrid laughs it off and says, "No problem, more for me."

After a couple more tunes, the guitar man takes a break and introduces himself to Jack. "You're Jack Thayer, aren't you?" Jack nods affirmative and shakes the guy's hand.

"I'm Lenny Sanders, and it's a pleasure meeting you. I have been a lifetime Wolverine fan and am excited about the upcoming season." Lenny glances at Mickey and goes on to say, "I see that you found your girl. She is very special, take good care of her."

Jack once again nods affirmative and replies, "I will do that. Is it true that you served three tours of combat overseas?"

Lenny nods "yes."

"Well then sir, it is I who is honored to meet you."

Lenny pats Jack on the shoulder and says, "I'll be rooting for you this year. I'm serious about you taking good care of that girl. I'll see you around Jack Thayer."

Lenny returns to his guitar and starts playing Uncle Kracker's, *Drift Away*. "*Give me the beat boys and free my soul, I want to get lost in your rock and roll and drift away!*"

While the foursome enjoy Lenny's singing, a boat comes towards the shore and anchors near the sandbar. A dozen partiers come running through the surf towards the bonfire and leading the pack is none other than the party boy, Rowdy.

Rowdy is greeted by the Rio kid who walks him to the bonfire. When the fire light illuminates Rowdy's face you can see that his eyes are bloodshot and glassed over. His apparent *friends* look like they are in the same condition. They are passing around a joint. Rowdy sees Jerrid and walks over and gives him a handshake hug. Rowdy reeks of marijuana. Jerrid laughs and jokingly greets him with, "Your Highness." Rowdy looks at Jerrid through his squinted eyes and laughs. Jack is not amused. He has a lot at stake and doesn't need to be around anyone using drugs.

Mickey pulls Jack away from the fire and speaks to him in a manner in which nobody else can hear. Jack nods his head in agreement and motions for Jerrid and Josie to come over to them. Jerrid asks, "What's up."

Jack states, "We've got to go, they have drugs at this party."

Jerrid wrinkles his face and retorts, "It's just weed. What's the big deal?"

Jack gives Jerrid a look that Mickey has not seen yet. He then responds, "Well, it's illegal and I am not going to jeopardize my football career at U of M or Mickey's volleyball career because I wasn't smart enough to leave. So Mickey and I are leaving. Are you coming along or are you staying?"

Jerrid is a little bigger than Jack, but everyone on the football team is quite aware of Jack's grit and sheer power. He is genuinely tough and not someone that you want to brace. Jack usually leads by example, but Jerrid was there when a defensive lineman threw Jack hard to the ground in practice. Jack got up and confronted the bigger lineman. When the lineman didn't back down and made a derogatory remark, Jack lowered his shoulder and rammed the guy in the gut, knocking him to the turf. He then jumped on top of him and applied some thump therapy. It took three other linemen to pull Jack off of the guy. Extremely embarrassed, the same guy approached Jack outside the practice facility and started running his mouth about Jack getting in a cheap shot. Jack walked over to the loud mouth and told him to take a shot. The lineman reared back and swung at Jack's head. Jack ducked, and followed up with a left-handed upper cut that knocked the bigger fellow to the ground. Jack stood over him and growled, "That was with my left hand. If you make me hit you with my throwing hand, I'll destroy you."

Knowing that Jack could do it, the lineman rubbed his chin and glared at Jack. Jack then surprised the big man by extending his right arm and lifted his teammate off the ground so that he could save face and walked him to his car.

Jerrid wants to stay at the party, but he knows that his best move is to avoid a conflict with Jack. After all, they are not only teammates, they work together, and he needs to support his partner's play whether he agrees with it or not.

Josie is not a fan of marijuana either, and she is glad that they are leaving. Josie's aunt, on her mother's side, has battled with drug addiction for over ten years, and she has regularly referred to marijuana as the *gateway drug.* Many people, including Josie's aunt, start by smoking pot, and then have the strong urge to progress to more serious drugs for an even higher high.

Rowdy sees the group leaving and heads them off before they start climbing the stairs to the jeep. "Hey, where are you going? I just got here. Don't leave me hanging. The party has just begun."

Jack gives Rowdy a stern look and replies, "We're out of here Rowdy. People are smoking marijuana, and we all have too much at stake to be caught up in this mess."

Rowdy cuts off Jack's path and gets up in his face. "When you say people, you actually mean me. I get the feeling that you don't like me very much, Jack!" Rowdy puts extra emphasis on Jack's name so that it sounds disrespectful.

By this time, a bunch of Rowdy's friends have gathered around and the tension starts to build. Jack steps aside to walk around Rowdy, and the bullheaded thug once again cuts him off. Rowdy gets a serious look on his face and retorts, "I'm one of the people smoking marijuana. Are you judging me?"

Jack takes a deep breath and looks to defuse the situation. After all, he has Mickey with him and her safety is his utmost concern. Jerrid steps up and says, "Don't personalize it, Rowdy. You do your thing and we'll do ours. We've made up our minds that we are going to go. Let's just leave it at that before someone says or does something that they will regret later."

Rowdy looks at the faces crowded around and he can tell that they are anticipating a fight. He is feeling the pressure of living up to his bad boy image. Rowdy likes Jerrid but his worth is on the line, and in his inebriated state he feels like Jack has dissed him. Like a cornered animal, his instinct is to strike out. Part of him wants to take on the quarterback stud. Rowdy likes to feel like the king of the hill but it is hard to do while you have a fellow of Jack's stature around.

Foolishly, Rowdy pushes Jack in the chest and calls him a punk. The shove knocks Jack back a half step back, but he quickly regains his ground. The determined look that Jerrid has seen so many times in competitive situations comes over Jack, and he knows that Jack is at his limit. Jerrid warns him, "Back off Rowdy, or you'll regret it!"

When Jack doesn't push back, Rowdy feels even more pressure to engage. This time he rears back to punch Jack. Before he can deliver the blow, Jack steps forward and delivers a strike with his left elbow that hits Rowdy squarely in the nose. Blood splatters from the broken nose and Rowdy bends over in pain. Jack then kicks Rowdy's legs out from under him which places him quickly on his back. The quick movements startle the on lookers and no one else poses a threat. Jack takes Mickey's hand and leads her up the hill to the safety of the jeep. Jerrid and Josie are right there with them and Jerrid keeps a watch on their back trail in case someone is stupid enough to pursue.

As Jack pulls onto the road he looks at Mickey and asks her if she is alright. Mickey assures him that she is and asks him if he hurt his arm striking the pothead. Jerrid chimes in, "I saw that you used your left arm to

deliver the blow. You didn't risk injuring your throwing hand. You're always one step ahead of the game. Hey man, I'm sorry for questioning you back there. You made the right call. It's too bad that Rowdy is such a jerk.
"

Jack thanks his friend for covering his back. He then asks him, "What's that term you use? It's buzzkill, isn't it?"

Jerrid laughs, "Yeah, that's it. I'd say it definitely applies to tonight."

Josie snuggles up to Jerrid in the back seat of the jeep. The night air has turned chilly and she is attempting to warm up.

When Jack drops Mickey off at Connie's, he once again walks her up to the door. Mickey sincerely looks him in the eyes and says, "I appreciate how you tried to diffuse the situation."

Jack says, "Your safety was my first concern. If I were to lose a little pride it would be alright as long as you remained safe. I'm sorry that you had to be there for that."

Mickey hugs him and says, "I also appreciate that you took that creep out. You defended yourself, and there is no shame to that!"

Mickey gives Jack a much longer kiss on this night before entering the cottage. "You're a good man, Jack Thayer, and I feel lucky to be with you."

As the door closes, Jack has emotions like none other before. Whether he is aware of it or not, he has fallen in love.

Chapter 18

Sundays have their own feel to them. For some, it's solely a day of recreation; for others, it is a day of rest and worship. Once again, Jack finds himself willfully walking with Mickey and Connie to the white church on the bluff. Lenny greets them at the door. He speaks to Jack privately, "I saw what happened last night. You did what you had to do, no shame in that. Are you alright?" Jack assures him that he is.

Lenny walks to the stage to accompany Connie with the music ministry. Jack sits proudly next to his girlfriend. A few minutes before the service, Josie walks down the middle aisle and sits in the pew on the other side of Mickey. Josie is acting sheepish, and her body language communicates that she is not at all comfortable. Mickey naturally picks up on it and slips her arm around her friend. Josie visibly relaxes as the worship leader walks up to the microphone.

When the music is done, the Reverend steps up to the podium to deliver his message. Today's sermon is based on the Bible verses found in Romans 3:23-24. *For all have sinned and fall short of the glory of God, and are justified freely by his grace through the redemption that came by Christ Jesus.* The pastor tells the story of Saul who persecuted and killed Christians. God changed his hardened heart and changed his name to Paul. Paul went on to faithfully serve God and wrote many of the books in the New Testament. At the end of the service, the pastor delivers an altar call and asks if anyone would like to step forward and accept Jesus into his or her heart and be saved. Unknown to Jack, Mickey and Connie have been praying for him.

The message has moved Jack and he feels a need to reply to the pastor's call. Jack takes a stand and walks down the aisle. The pastor leads Jack and five others in the sinner's prayer. "Dear Jesus, I acknowledge that you are Lord and Savior. I admit that I have sinned and am in need of salvation. Please forgive me of my sins and accept me into your kingdom. Thank you, amen."

Jack feels like a giant weight has been lifted off of his shoulders, and he is genuinely at peace. When he turns around, he sees that Mickey is standing right behind him with tears running down her face. She embraces him in a big hug. Connie tries to play the piano while her own eyes glass over with tears. Connie looks to the heavens and mouths, "Thank you, Lord!"

After the service Mickey invites Josie over for dinner, but Josie respectively declines saying, "I have to get home. Besides, I think that I'd feel like a third wheel. You go and enjoy your time with Jack. I'll see you tomorrow night at the beach."

Barbecue chicken is on the menu today, and once again Jack mans the grill. He douses the charred bird with Sweet Baby Ray's Barbeque Sauce. Mickey and Connie definitely have a new pep to their step. God is good!

Chapter 19

Rowdy is sitting at the bar nursing a beer. His nose is swollen and his head is throbbing. He would normally still be in bed, but he has another appointment that he must keep. Fifteen minutes after one, another man sits down on the stool next to him and orders a beer. The Detroit Tigers are playing on a flat screen television, and the two men engage in small talk concerning the Tigers. Miguel Cabrera is having another stellar season.

The only other person in the bar is Lenny. He is eating steak at a table in the corner watching the game. Shortly after the stranger sits down, Lenny excuses himself and reaches in between the two men and grabs a handful of napkins. Apparently, he has spilled his water. Rowdy and the stranger don't even notice the recording device that Lenny sticks to the napkin holder.

In between observations on the Tigers, Rowdy and the stranger finalize plans for a shipment of heroin. Historically, the stranger has hired *mules* to transport the drug from Chicago to Benton Harbor by stashing it in secret compartments in automobiles. Lately, the Drug Enforcement Agency (DEA) has made a high number of busts on Interstate-94, which in turn is cutting deeply into the drug lord's profits. He now wants to run the drugs over the water, and Rowdy has been chosen for the task. The Chicago man wants to bypass Benton Harbor and distribute the drugs from South Haven.

Rowdy is an adrenaline junkie and views it as a daring adventure. He is also sucked in by the money. Three beers later, the Tigers win 7 – 5 over the New York Yankees. The plan for the drug run is finalized. The stranger leaves and five minutes later Rowdy departs. He is looking forward to going back to bed and escaping the throbbing headache that his broken nose has caused. Once the men have left, Lenny returns to the bar and retrieves the recording device. The DEA uses the best technology available!

Chapter 20

What a great day. Mickey has sold over $500 of her own art. People who hate their jobs complain about Mondays, but Mickey has discovered that Mondays are a good sale day at the gallery. She is in an extra good mood. Her high priced piece has not yet been sold, but Connie keeps reminding her to have faith and declares that it will sell before the summer is over. Connie tells her this with such conviction that she is starting to become a believer.

After work, Mickey drives to North Beach to meet up with her volleyball partner. As usual, the girls start with stretching and then proceed to their passing drill. Josie is quiet and obviously distracted. Mickey can't read her mind, but she gives her friend space thinking that if she has something to say that she will come out with it. After all, Josie has never been shy.

The girls are challenged to a game by another team and they happily welcome the competition. Josie serves an ace for game point and they beat the other girls 21 – 5. Mickey and Josie keep the court, and the next challengers are a co-ed team that has a short guy and what appears to be his girlfriend. They are not much of a challenge, and the girls smoke them 21 – 2. Mickey and Josie each make a bad serve giving the other team their only points. They are about to leave when another co-ed team challenges them. This time they have a competitive game but they still win 21 – 14.

After practice the girls get ice cream cones and eat in silence. Mickey decides to speak up and tells Josie about her good sales day. Josie politely nods her head,

77

but in reality her mind is a million miles away. Mickey is outright concerned so she asks her friend, "What's going on?

Josie is staring out over the big Great Lake when Mickey asks the question and doesn't even hear her. Mickey shakes her friends arm to bring her back to reality. "Josie, what's going on?"

Josie's lips move but nothing comes out. She wants to talk but she can't get the words out. Mickey looks her friend in the eyes and says, "Tell me Josie, what's bothering you?"

Just as Josie is about to say something, Jack and Jerrid come running up from behind the girls and tap them on their shoulders and yell out, "You're it." They keep on running towards the lake. Josie takes off after them and Mickey quickly follows. The boys run out into the surf and dive in once the water reaches their waist. Josie beats Mickey into the water by a couple of strides, but they both end up diving into the surf at the same time. When they bob up out of the water, they see that Jack has a Frisbee and a game of catch develops. Mickey steals a look at her friend to see how she is doing and it appears like all is well. Josie catches the Frisbee and intentionally throws it over Jerrid's head making him chase it into deeper water. The girl just loves to play. The game of catch goes on for close to an hour. After the game, Jack suggests that they walk the pier to dry off. Jack holds Mickey's hand and Jerrid follows his lead and reaches out for Josie's.

While walking the pier, Rowdy's boat is moving through the channel. This time he doesn't have his usual entourage. There is only one other passenger and he is looking in the other direction. Rowdy notices Jack and flips him the bird. Jerrid shakes his head in disgust and says, "And I thought that guy was our friend."

Jack chuckles and says, "Apparently he is no friend of mine."

The boat passes and the happy couples walk to the end of the pier. They sit with their feet dangling over the edge. As everyone sits quietly, Jack blurts out, "Common denominator."

Mickey looks confused and asks Jack what he is referring to. Jack says, "The lake, it's something we all have in common."

Everyone nods in agreement. The large expanse of water mixed with a good supply of sand and sunshine soothes the soul. Josie rests her head on Jerrid's shoulder. For three of the four the world is as it should be, but for Josie, her world has been rocked. She is filled with conflicting emotions. Eventually she will talk about it, but for now her mind is swimming, and she needs time to clear her head. Life is often a roller coaster ride with highs and lows and sometimes the ride is just too freaking fast!

Chapter 21

At the break of dawn, Lenny Sanders, rides his Harley Davidson Fatboy down M-43 towards Kalamazoo. Just as the sun begins to rise from the horizon, Lenny pulls into a Denny's Restaurant for a Grand Slam breakfast. When Lenny walks through the front door, he sees Dan sitting at a booth drinking coffee. Lenny sits down across from him and Dan greets him with the customary good morning greeting, except he calls him by a different name, "Good morning Noah."

Noah returns the pleasantry, "Good morning, Dan."

Lenny Sanders is Noah's undercover name. The undercover officers pick out their own names. Since Noah's undercover job is that of the guitar player, he chose Lenny which is the nickname for Lynyrd in honor of his father's favorite band, Lynyrd Skyryrd. Sanders, is a tribute to one of his all-time favorite football players, Barry Sanders, the former Detroit Lion who is arguably the best running back to have ever played the game.

Noah gives Dan the recording that he made at the bar of Rowdy's conversation with the man from Chicago. When Noah listened to the recording, he discovered that Rowdy has scheduled to make a drug run this upcoming Friday.

Since Noah works at the bar playing guitar, he was also able to get the video footage of the Chicago man when he entered and left the bar. Noah sent this footage electronically to Dan and he was able to find out that the man's name is Franco. Franco is connected to the same drug traffickers who were previously making their runs via the interstate.

Because the DEA rarely makes busts on the very first shipment, Franco wants to gamble and make an exceptionally large shipment on this inaugural trip. Franco is going to have a woman get on board Rowdy's boat in Chicago, so that it looks like he is picking up a passenger. He intends to load her carry-on bag with two bricks of heroin. Franco has also surmised that it will look less conspicuous if Rowdy has a beautiful woman with him, rather than him riding all alone.

Noah and Dan both agree that the best place to ambush the boat will be when it returns to the marina. There is too much risk out on the open water. They can control the environment at the boat docks. In addition, this will prove that the shipment is intended for southern Michigan and will hopefully work as a deterrent for anybody thinking about running drugs through the marina in the future.

Dan tells Noah that he is aware of Rowdy's affiliation to the U of M basketball team, and he is also aware that two other U of M athletes are using a boat at the same marina. Dan asks Noah if he thinks they are working together. Noah relates the incident at the party and shares that he was surveying the pier when Rowdy flipped off Jack. On top of that, he saw that Jack committed his life to God on Sunday. Jack is a definite no! Jerrid, he is not sure, but if he was a betting man, he would vote no there as well.

Noah learns that four police officers chartered the fishing boat a couple of weeks ago when it was first learned that drug runners planned on utilizing a boat from the South Haven marina. They ruled out Jack and

Jerrid's involvement, but identified Rowdy as a target. Even though his defendant history report indicates no prior felonies they were able to find out that there were drug offenses in High School that his daddy's attorney got dismissed. A felonious assault of a police officer charge was pled down to a misdemeanor and that charge still shows up on the LEIN (Law Enforcement Information Network).

Before Noah returns to South Haven, he and Dan formulate a plan for the ambush at the marina. The plan is for the drug task force team to meet at the high school parking lot on the day of the bust to finalize their preparations. This type of bust can be a career builder within the DEA. Noah is stoked; he experienced the same rush on missions overseas. Like Rowdy, he too is an adrenaline junkie, but he prefers to stay on the right side of the law!

Chapter 22

"You haven't experienced the Fourth of July until you have spent the national holiday in a beach town," Stephanie says to a tourist visiting from Indianapolis, Indiana. Stephanie is volunteering for the Chamber of Commerce and is working at the information booth located along the walkway leading to South Beach. The tourist is a lady in her thirties who is trying to corral her three young children while holding a conversation. She is totally pleased with her visit and is seeking further information.

"Is there an art gallery in town? I would like to take something back as a reminder of this wonderful place." Stephanie sets a map of the town on the top of her booth and marks the location for the *Great Lake Expressions* gallery.

"Thank you," replies the anxious mother. She no longer turns around when a major crisis happens. At least it is from the perspective of a child. Her youngest, who looks to be about four, loses the top of his ice cream cone and starts to cry as the strawberry flavored delight splatters on the sidewalk.

The Fourth of July, is in its very essence, the signature of summer. American flags adorn every little store and the landscape becomes a sea of red, white and blue. *The Children's Store* sells a wide assortment of patriotic colored shirts that showcase an American flag in the forefront of a sunlit shoreline. South Haven, USA, reads across the bottom. It seems like every kid in town ends up owning one of the collector shirts. It also seems like every child ends up dripping ice cream on their new shirts because you can't make it through the day without stopping at one of the several shops that serve the delicious dessert. Parents indulge right along with their offspring because after all, it would be un-American not to!

Amplified music can be heard coming from the direction of the band shell as a local band plays songs from the 90's. July 4th competes as one of the busiest business days of the summer. Thousands of people descend on the small community to watch the annual firework show that takes place out over the lake.

As Stephanie talks to a lady who is interested in finding the closest restroom, she notices four guys walking towards her. Leading the group is a muscular long haired guy and his entourage of hero worshipers. Rowdy and his pack of misspent youth are up to no good, and they take great pleasure in making fun of people as they walk towards the beach.

Stephanie recognizes one of the boys in the group as being the one who talked her into doing the line of cocaine. She was really hoping that she would never see him again. At the time of her misdeed, she had thought that he was cute. She wanted to remain in his good graces, so against her better judgment, she went ahead and partook of the dangerous drug. Out of all her regrets in life, this decision ranks at the top.

As fate would have it, Rowdy leads his group of friend's right up to Stephanie's booth. He looks at Stephanie with an amused look and says, "Excuse me, but do your ankles hurt? Because it looks like you have just fallen from heaven"

Rowdy's friends howl at the cheesy line, and Stephanie's face turns red from a combination of sheer anger and embarrassment. Being the butt of the joke is the last thing she needs.

Before she can reply, another volunteer comes to her aid. It's Coach Granger, and he runs the boys off before they can inflict any more damage. As they walk away, Stephanie overhears the boy who gave her the drug say to Rowdy, "Dude, that's the chick who overdosed at your pool."

Rowdy looks back over his shoulder and shrugs, "Wow, I totally forgot about her."

Stephanie is dumbfounded. What's more absurd? Rowdy's inhumane behaviors or the fact that he of all people has a following. His total indifference further reminds Stephanie that she never, ever wants to take another illegal drug for the rest of her life. She prays silently in her head, "Thank you Lord for watching over me. You are a great God! Please keep me strong."

When Stephanie looks back up, she smiles when she sees Mickey and Josie's happy faces. Mickey gives her a hug and she asks, "What are you two doing here? Mickey, I just sent someone to your gallery, aren't you open?

Mickey replies, "Yeah, we're open. Connie's covering while I take my lunch break. We've come by here to see if you would like to go to the concert with us tonight. Jack and Jerrid are playing in a celebrity golf outing so we are having a girls night out. What do you say? Are you in?"

"Yeah, I'm in, where do you want to meet?'

Josie says, "Let's all meet at Connie's at six. Frankie Ballard is headlining tonight's show. It should be a lot of fun!"

Chapter 23

Every year the U of M alumni have a Fourth of July golf tournament, and the head football and basketball coaches are expected to make an appearance and mingle with the boosters. Included in the group is the owner of *The Wolverine*, Mr. Garrison.

Considering that they will be team captains for the upcoming season, Thayer and Stone are also on the *expected* list. It's not a bad gig. You get to golf for free and hang with some of the former players. Jack is looking forward to talking with Tom Brady if given the chance. Jerrid is more concerned about disguising his beer. He has successfully poured some into an empty Vernors bottle. This is a pretty foolish move. Risking a full-paid scholarship to a school as prestigious as the University of Michigan seems insane to Jack. Jerrid pacifies himself with the rationale that there are many players doing much worse. Cocaine and speed are used by some of the other guys. At least he is not doing anything illegal, especially now that he is twenty-one.

Jack gets teamed up with three Ford Motor Company executives. Fortunately, these three men are good golfers and equally good at holding a conversation. Of course, they want to discuss the Ohio State rivalry and talk about their own glory days on the gridiron. The oldest gentlemen tells the group that he was an All-State quarterback back in the day, but his 5' 11" height and weak knees kept him from playing at the collegiate level.

"Hey Jack, are we going to beat Ohio State this year?"

Jack quickly retorts, "Is the F150 the best pick-up in America? Of course we are going to beat Oh-How-I-Hate-Ohio-State!"

The executives laugh out loud and grow even fonder of their team's starting quarterback. Jack knows that the men want to see confidence, if not outright cockiness, from their team leader, and he is happy to oblige. After all, it's not an act; he fully believes that they will beat the Buckeyes and every other team on the schedule.

The executives love their alcohol and indulge whenever the beer cart appears. Jack remains loyal to his daily intake of bottled water. Jack has wrongly assumed that these men were in their late fifties when in fact he learns that they are actually in their early-forties. The stress of their high profile jobs combined with a reliance on alcohol has really taken its toll.

****

The three girls have found a spot close to the stage and are now singing along to Frankie's first hit *"Tell Me You Get Lonely."* Live music in the open air is always great, but when done in close proximity to Lake Michigan, it is pure magic. Frankie is from Mickey's hometown, Battle Creek, Michigan. He has just come off of a tour where he opened for another Michigan superstar, Bob Seger. Frankie notices Mickey in the audience and brings her and her friends on stage for his next song *"A Bunch of Girls."*

The girls dance along to the tune and Josie is in her glory. She feels like a rock goddess and seizes the moment. Frankie walks over to serenade the trio and quickly picks up on Josie's showmanship by engaging her with playful antics. She is a natural and the crowd goes wild.

After the song, security leads the girls off stage, and all three of them have their phones blow up with text messages. One of Stephanie's friends has taken a video of the event and has already sent it to her. Stephanie forwards the link to Josie and Mickey and they send it to Jerrid and Jack. Mickey attaches a message "Wish you were here!"

When the concert is over, the girls move from the bandstand to the beach. Darkness has moved in and the coveted fireworks are about to be lit. The only thing that could make the night any better for Mickey is to have Jack here with her. She is surprised at how much she misses him. She knows that she is falling in love but is scared to death to say it out loud. She doesn't want to jinx a good thing.

A loud BOOM lets the crowd of people know that the fireworks have begun. The bright colorful display of aerial lights is simply spectacular. July 4th has always been Stephanie's favorite holiday. This was probably developed from a lifetime of celebrating the holiday at the lake. What a great way of capping off a terrific day.

As the girls head out from the beach, Rowdy and his entourage of what Mickey would label *thugs* walk up alongside them. Rowdy shows a disgusting favor towards Josie and is quick to hit on her. "Hey gorgeous, I saw you on stage dancing tonight. Why don't you come back to my place and *dance* with me?"

Josie gives him a disgusted look and replies, "No, I don't think so."

Rowdy doesn't like the word "no" and places his arm around her waist, "Come on, have some fun."

Josie twists out of his arms and becomes angry with the aggressive move. "I said no you jerk, now leave me alone."

Rowdy seems undeterred and laughs at her. He is about to grab her arm when he notices a policeman up ahead and leads his group quickly away. He is gone as fast as he appeared. What a creep. The girls hustle towards home before the jerk reappears.

Chapter 24

Heads turn when Mickey and Jack cruise up in his black jeep wrangler. Freshly washed and waxed, the jeep still doesn't shine as bright as the smiles displayed on the beautiful couple riding in it. This Friday night, the church's youth and young adult ministry have sponsored a beach party for church members and their friends. Coolers packed with pop, juice and water are readily available as well as hotdogs and the fixings for s'mores. Jack and Mickey fit the stereotype of an all-American couple. Everyone is aware of their status as collegiate athletes and many are anxious to engage the two in conversation. Mickey notices Stephanie and embraces her with a hug.

After brief small talk, Stephanie sheepishly asks Mickey, "I was wondering, could we possibly get together some night? I would love it if you could help me get better at volleyball. I play on the high school team and I could use some pointers."

Mickey nods her head yes and asks, "What position do you play?"

Stephanie responds, "Middle-hitter."

Mickey once again nods her approval and says, "Let's meet at North Beach, Monday night around 6 o'clock. I usually work out with Josie, but I'm sure that the two of us could give you some pointers."

Stephanie laughs nervously and responds, "Alright, I'll be there."

With that being said, Jack grabs three hotdogs and places them on a "cooking stick" and says to Mickey,

"Hey, I'll cook up three dogs if you and Stephanie prepare the buns, deal?"

Mickey nods yes and the two girls grab paper plates and prep the buns with ketchup, mustard and relish. Mickey purposely leaves the onions off because she is quite confident that she will kiss Jack later in the evening.

Once again the South Haven sun sets in a spectacular fashion. After the youthful appetites grub on hotdogs and chips, they naturally choose to cap off their meal with the delicious campfire treat called the s'more. Jack lamely jokes, "I've had them before, but now I want *some more.*"

The girls roll their eyes and hand him three marshmallows to roast while they break up Hershey candy bars and place them on squared graham crackers. Stephanie is quite pleased to be included within their inner-circle. She looks up to Mickey. The girl is just real.

When Jack takes his last bite from his s'more, he sees Lenny walking towards the fire with guitar in hand. Lenny is wearing a long sleeved, light blue shirt with a surfing logo. The long sleeves are pushed up past his elbows and a military tattoo is clearly visible on his tanned left forearm. Jack greets Lenny with a firm handshake. Lenny says, "Good to see you here. I talked the management at the Jolly Roger into doing karaoke tonight so that I could be here. Truth of the matter is, this is more of my kind of crowd than the clientele at the bar. I would much rather gather with the saints than the ain'ts, just saying."

Jack point blank asks Lenny if he is a Christian. Lenny chuckles and says, "There are no atheists in foxholes. When you spend time on the battlefield you take a serious look at the purpose of life. Most soldiers believe in God and ask for His protection, but then they turn away from Him and what He wants from them once the fighting is over. Like most others, I prayed for His protection while fighting the war. But now that I am safely home, I intend to live the life that He has intended for me. Our life on earth is but a single drop of water compared to this huge lake. I want to make the most of mine!"

Lenny sits down and tunes his guitar while Jack ponders what his friend has just said. There's that theme again; purpose of life. Jack is feeling really content. He headed into the summer only thinking about sex and having a good time. Instead, he is dating a virgin and seeking the company of *church people*. Ironically, he is having the time of his life. Life provides a lot of twists and turns. It's up to the individual whether it's going to be lemons or lemonade.

Mickey's enthusiasm is contagious. Jack has developed a serious zest for life. His thirst for learning about God can't be quenched. He now reads the Bible on a daily basis and is astonished at the wisdom and inspiration that lies in the written Word. Men of integrity abound in story after story. Jesus' disciples willingly give up their lives to follow the leader and his profound teachings. The life of Christ amazes him and he understands why so many choose to be Christians, or as the Word defines, to be Christ like.

Lenny is hungry and quickly downs a couple hotdogs. As he finishes off his second dog, two young men stoke the fire by adding large driftwood logs. The fire leaps for the heavens. The group circles the towering inferno. Lenny and a female youth leader lead the group in songs about God. Included are *Oceans, Our God, Mighty to Save, Revelation Song* and the powerful *10,000 Reasons*. No one in this group is too cool for school. Everyone sings along with true sincerity. Seeing is believing and Jack witnesses that everyone gathered around the fire has one *common denominator*; a strong love for God.

****

Across town, Josie is with Jerrid. He has taken her to another beach party where there is also a bonfire, but the main theme here seems to be beer. Jerrid is consuming more than his fair share and is really getting hammered. Josie can't help but notice that their *dates* always involve alcohol followed up with a night of sex. Romance and conversation no longer exist. Jerrid tends to be very moody until he gets a *couple* of beers in him.

At one point, Jerrid is refilling at the keg and is gone longer than usual. Josie feels bored so she takes a walk down to the beach. The starlit sky is calming, as are the waves that splash ashore. She has a lot on her mind and knows that she needs to have a serious talk with Jerrid, but she is unsure of what to say. Many questions fog her mind. Does she love him? Does she even like him? What are his feelings for her or, for that matter, does he even have feelings for her? Is she just his *plaything*?

While these thoughts and many others are twirling in her mind, someone quietly walks up behind her and places his hands on her waist. Josie thinks to herself, "He does care for me; he came and found me." She turns to face him and is startled when she sees that it isn't Jerrid. It's Rowdy!

Josie attempts to escape his grip, but Rowdy displays a devilish grin, pulls her in tight to him and tries to kiss her. "Hello babe, let's finish what we started a few days ago."

Josie tries to fight him off, but the muscular athlete is very strong. Fear takes hold and Josie is scared. Rowdy tries to force her to the ground, but Josie fights off his unwanted advance and remains on her feet. Josie is about to scream when she hears Jerrid yell, "Hey, get away from her!"

Rowdy ignores Jerrid and tries to kiss Josie while holding her tight against his body. Josie sees that his eyes are glassed over and knows that he is higher than a kite. Her fear turns to anger and she thrust her head forward, head-butting the jerk on his injured nose. Once again blood splatters and a surge of pain forces Rowdy to release his grip. Josie takes off running back towards the fire, but Jerrid pounces on Rowdy and knocks him to the ground. Jerrid pounds Rowdy with a series of blows which strike his face. He is inflicting serious damage, so a group of guys intervene. It ends up taking five guys to remove the enraged athlete off Rowdy, but they manage to do so. Their actions save Rowdy's life.

Jerrid flees the scene, returns to the bonfire and searches for Josie. She is gone. Sirens can be heard advancing towards the party so Jerrid decides to flee. Josie has been rescued by a former high school classmate who offers to take her home. Josie buries her head into her hands and sobs. She is scared and doesn't know who to turn to.

The police arrive and determine that Rowdy needs to be transported by ambulance to the hospital. He is unconscious and his face is a bloody mess. Blood coats his long blond hair. Most of the partiers have left the scene and those who remain behind claim to know nothing about the fight. The police officer pulls a wallet out of the injured man's pants and finds an I.D. The name registers in the officer's mind. He has targeted Rob as a possible drug user. The cop thinks to himself, "live by the sword, die by the sword."

Chapter 25

Jerrid's right hand is swollen and bruised. He is also nursing a serious hangover from his night of heavy drinking. It's hard for him to say what hurts worst, his hand or his head. Jack has mixed feelings concerning his friend. On one hand, he wishes that he was at the party to have had Jerrid's back and yet on the other hand, he knows that Jerrid is drinking too much and is his own worst enemy. Previous discussions on the matter have not gone very well, so Jack is naturally hesitant to bring up the hot topic. Jerrid's dad and uncles are heavy drinkers and it is like an unwritten passage of manhood in their family. Every family event revolves around alcohol. Building up a strong alcohol tolerance level is considered a badge of honor.

Jack understands that Rowdy's behavior is out of control and that Jerrid did what he had to do; but he can't help but wonder if Jerrid hadn't been drinking, might he have handled it with a little more rational thinking before beating the sorry son of a gun into a near coma. A day of fishing will be good medicine for his troubled friend. There are a lot of references to water being a source of healing and for these two rugged outdoorsmen, there is nothing finer than time spent out on Lake Michigan.

Another gorgeous day is experienced offshore. Today's clients include four academic gentlemen, all of whom are college professors. The two oldest men are professors at Hope College and they are hosting two friends who teach at Calvin College. Quite pleasing to Jack is the fact that these four men are all Christian and speak openly about their faith. The eldest professor, Mr.

Alexandrian, starts the day's conversation sharing about a public debate that he recently had with an atheist about the historical evidence of the life of Christ. He brought up archeological findings and spoke with great clarity about their significance. He also brought up many confirmed books that came from the same era of time which confirm much of what is written in the Bible.

Jerrid went about his daily work in silence only speaking when he needed to do so. Jack on the other hand was all ears and soaked up the information like a sponge. Much to the pleasure of the professors, he showed a genuine interest in their topic and asked questions when it was appropriate to do so.

Eventually the conversation went to the topic of how Jesus life had fulfilled numerous prophecies that had been previously recorded in the Old Testament book of Isaiah. For once, fishing was like the secondary activity for the day. Oh sure, the professors are having a great time catching fish, but they equally enjoy each other's company and eagerly re-engage in their spirited conversations about God and the Bible.

Today's trip went by much too fast for Jack. The lively discussion made time fly by. As usual, Jerrid displays the fish so that the clients can have a souvenir photograph. Once again the clients had arrived as complete strangers, but leave as new friends. Jack absolutely loves this job!

After the men have left, Jack and Jerrid clean up the boat and organize the gear. As they do this, two college aged girls approach their boat on Sea-Doo's and boldly asks them if they want to go for a ride. Both of the guys have been wanting to ride Sea-Doo's on the Great Lake so they gladly accept the invitation. The girls scoot back on their two person seats allowing for the guys to drive.

It takes a little while to navigate the slow pace of the Black River. When they eventually hit the open water of Lake Michigan, a fun time is quickly at hand. Jumping the swells is fun and challenging with two people on each Sea-Doo but the girls are as adventurous as the guys, so they do not object. Jack is having a blast. They ride in the open water for a fun filled hour or more until Jerrid hits one particularly big swell and flies the watercraft high into the air and dumps his passenger into the drink. This stunt brings an end to the fun.

It is decided that it would be best to return to *The Wolverine*. When they get back to the boat the girls invite the guys to their cottage for a drink. Jack respectively declines, but much to his surprise, Jerrid takes them up on the offer and gets back on the Sea-Doo that he was driving. The girl who was riding with Jack displays a pouty face and says, "Come on, please."

Jerrid fires the Sea-Doo back up and yells out, "You snooze, you lose" while motoring the watercraft away from the dock.

Jerrid and the girl ride off. The second girl then says, "Come on over, I guarantee you won't regret it!"

Sexual temptation is staring Jack right smack in the face with a bikini clad girl. When Jack doesn't reply, she jumps up onto the dock and boldly says, "Or I can stay right here with you."

The Holy Spirit comes over Jack and he remembers a verse that he has recently read in 1st Corinthians that says, *"Run from sexual immorality."* Jack grabs the keys to his jeep and says, "I've got to go." He then takes off running in the direction of the parking lot.

Chapter 26

Mickey and Josie have entered the beach volleyball tournament in St. Joseph. This town is twenty-seven miles south of South Haven. The Silver Beach tournament has a later start, and because the girls are seeded high, they do not have to play their first game until 11 a.m. Mickey takes the rare opportunity to sleep in. Josie on the other hand has had a restless night so she is once again dragging. Mornings have not been treating her well. She has decided that she is going to confide with her good friend a secret that she has been hiding. She has wanted to tell her earlier but has been afraid to talk about it because then her issue would be all that much more real.

When Mickey pulls in the driveway, Josie is surprised to see that she has brought Stephanie. Right away, Josie decides to table her much over-due conversation for another time. Stephanie jumps into the back seat so that the older girl can have the front seat. Stephanie is quite aware of Josie's talent and knows that she has the South Haven high school record for most kills in a season. Josie's phone vibrates and it's a text message from Jerrid. She chooses to ignore it and shuts off her phone. She needs to focus on volleyball and communicating with Jerrid right now is not a wise option. She has a mixed bag of emotions concerning him. She is hurt, confused, disappointed and if she must admit it, outright angry!

Josie has good social skills and engages Stephanie in small talk about her volleyball ambitions. The ride is quick and Stephanie is in her glory. She now eats, sleeps and dreams volleyball and here she is hanging with two of the best. Stephanie is high-spirited and her enthusiasm is contagious. She actually reminds Josie of a younger Mickey. Stephanie would be thrilled to hear such praise, but Josie keeps this thought to herself.

The girls coast through the first two games of the tournament with easy victories. Josie is punishing the ball with some of the fiercest serves and spikes that Mickey has ever witnessed from her partner . Josie has transferred stored up anger onto the volleyball court and it is working wonders. Once again the girls take the tournament title and are donned Queens of the Beach! Stephanie cheers loudly for the champions as they are recognized on the winner's platform and covets the opportunity of one day being up there herself.

The three girls have a spirited ride home. They remove their headbands and pony tail holders and let their long hair dance in the wind. All three of them sing along to a Miranda Lambert CD. The three girls feel every bit as feisty as the sassy blond country singer.

Chapter 27

Rob doesn't wake up until late into the afternoon. Through blurry eyes he sees that he is in a hospital bed with IV's pumping fluids into his arms. His long hair is matted in blood, his head aches and his jaw is extremely sore. He explores his mind to see why he is here. His memory returns to Friday night. He pictures the beautiful brunette at the beach. He then remembers someone yelling at him. It's Jerrid, and then his mind reminds him of the quick beating that Jerrid put on him. The linebacker's fist felt like sledgehammers. After the first two quick blows he was completely defenseless.

Nurse Roberts walks by the room and sees Rob stirring in his bed. He looks confused so she walks over to his bed. Rob's eyes focus on Donna, and before he can speak she says, "Don't try to talk. It's best if you just relax. You took quite a beating. I'll alert the doctor that you are awake. He wants to talk to you.'

Donna walks towards the nursing station and the words linger in Rob's brain. He remembers the brunette head-butting him in the face and rightly concludes that his nose has been re-broken. One of the IV's is actually a morphine drip, but it is putting a small dent on his pain threshold. Before Donna returns, Rob slips back asleep.

The DEA is informed of Rob's hospitalization. They had already pinged his cell phone and this alerted them that he was there for an extended period of time. Rob's prognosis is not good and they don't believe that the drug run will be conducted as originally planned. Like most happenings in the criminal world, unforeseen circumstances intervene and delay what looked to be a slam-dunk drug bust. Word is relayed to Lenny and he will further monitor the underground criminal element in what most others view as a paradise.

The Chicago drug lords are curious as to why they have not heard from Rob. They send one of their foot soldiers to South Haven to see if Rowdy Rob has gotten cold feet. Within an hour of arriving at the beach town, the man hears that Rob is in the hospital. Word travels fast in the small town. Ironically, the South Haven police also know what happened, but no one will come forward with first-hand information because either they don't want to get involved or for the added fact that most feel that Rowdy deserved what he got. The Old Testament logic of *an eye for an eye and a tooth for a tooth* takes a quick hold on the mindset of those who witnessed the ordeal. Rowdy crossed the line when he tried to force himself on Josie. Rowdy Rob is now *facing* the consequences!

Chapter 28

Sun tanned bodies linger late into the evening on this gorgeous summer night. North Beach is a happening place. Mickey, Josie and Stephanie pass the volleyball back and forth and as usual, older boys and young men awkwardly attempt to steal glances with less than subtle looks. Wearing mirrored Oakleys, Josey notices a twenty something guy checking her out. She finds herself strongly attracted to the tanned admirer. Conflicting thoughts rise up again. Where are things going with Jerrid? Is she committed to him or for that matter is he to her? Would this new admirer like her for more than her looks? Lots of guys look, but do they like who she really is?

Mickey on the other hand doesn't even pay attention to the gawkers. In her world, life is easy. She likes Jack and she is confident that he likes her. If not, then God will give her the desire of her heart because she is living in accordance to His will. It definitely hurt when her last boyfriend left her, but now with the passage of time she clearly sees that he was not *the one* meant for her. Mickey puts her trust in God and she feels that He has truly blessed her life. She puts a lot of stock in the verse from Romans which states, *"If God is for us, who can be against us?"*

Both Mickey and Josie offer pointers to the younger Stephanie. She is a good student and eagerly accepts their instruction. After an hour of performing various volleyball drills, Josie calls for a game. She enlists the tanned gawker as her partner and allows Mickey and Stephanie to team up against them. As it turns out the gawker's name is Steve and he has game. In the first game, Mickey and Stephanie win a tight battle 21 – 18. In the second game, Josie and her partner win by the same score. They decide to call it a draw and do not have a third game. Steve asks for Josie's number, but after a brief hesitation, she declines stating, "I'm kind of seeing someone."

Steve accepts the brushoff and returns to his friends. Stephanie puts in a strong performance and both girls are quick to praise her. The teenager is beaming with pride and sheepishly accepts the praise. She has to get home, but she thanks Mickey and Josie for including her in the night's workout and games.

When Stephanie drives off, Josie and Mickey collect their things. Josie catches Mickey's eye and says, "I need to have that talk with you. Why don't we get in your jeep and drive to the bluff that overlooks South Beach."

Mickey nods her head in agreement. She has observed that Josie has been tackling something rather heavy for a couple of weeks now and is eager to get to the bottom of it.

The girls ride silently across the bridge and back through town. Josie is deep in thought debating on what words to use. Mickey senses Josie's anxiety and prays a silent prayer asking God for the wisdom and words needed to comfort her friend.

After Mickey parks the jeep, the girls walk over to a public bench that sits high upon the bluff overlooking the magnificent Great Lake. At first Josie just stares out over the water. Tears form in her eyes and one of them drops onto her tanned legs. She looks at her friend and then the dam bursts. Tears stream down her face and she blurts out, "Mickey, I'm pregnant!"

Mickey obviously senses the distress that her friend is feeling and sympathy tears form in her eyes as well. She just listens. Josie goes on, "I have been getting sick every morning and I am three weeks late for my period. At first, I thought that I was just hung over from drinking beer with Jerrid, but I stopped drinking with him and continued being sick in the mornings."

Josie continues to cry. Mickey hugs her friend and gently places Josie's head on her shoulder and allows her friend to cry. Josie has been bottling it up and now that her emotions are coming out she is sobbing uncontrollably. Mickey's loving spirit is soothing.

Josie then sits up and says, "I don't know what to do. I'm scared to tell my mom and I'm scared to tell Jerrid. I'm confused if I really like him or if he likes me. I had such high expectations for the upcoming volleyball season and now this door will suddenly be closed. I've let my teammates down and I have let myself down. This was supposed to be our year. I have totally screwed up and I am scared. Yes, I am scared."

The tears keep pouring out and Mickey continues to comfort her hurting friend. Mickey kindly asks, "Have you been to a doctor yet?"

Josie shakes her head and responds, "No, but I did take a home pregnancy test. You know, one of those pee on the stick tests and it came back positive. I am pregnant and I am scared!"

As the South Haven sun sets, hundreds of people take it in and smile with joy. Two young ladies fail to notice the night's spectacular event. One carries a heavy heart while the other passionately tends to her distraught friend.

Chapter 29

Crazy and fear don't often mix, but after being thumped twice, Rowdy wants to steer clear of Jack and Jerrid. His face can't take any more blows. A near death experience can put fear into even the craziest of people.

Rowdy's thumbs work the keypad of his phone and he texts his contact in Chicago that he has been discharged from the hospital. The man in Chicago texts back and ask for another meeting at the bar. Unknown to Rowdy, Lenny has gotten a court order and is reading every text sent and received from his phone. Lenny will have the bar bugged prior to the meeting to gather as much intelligence as he can. Not only does Lenny want to catch Rowdy in the act, but he and the other agents believe that they will be able to get Rowdy to roll on the distributor for southwest Michigan. This is who they are after. Rowdy is just a punk kid in over his head.

Lenny reports the new information up the chain of command. Since the meeting is a couple of days away, he has some time to kill and he decides to go for a motorcycle ride on the outskirts of town. Orchards dot the landscape and there are quite a few roadside stands selling the tasty blueberries that the area is famous for. Temptation gets the better of him and Lenny stops by one of the stands and buys a pint of the fresh berries. They make for a healthy mid-day snack.

When Lenny returns to town, he stops by *Great Lake Expressions.* The gallery has caught his eye and his curious nature prompts him to stop. Lenny's mother was an artist. She sold her art work at a west coast gallery where he grew up in southern California. Lenny's mother worked with clay and would make ornate southwestern pottery. Lenny was always fascinated with the canvas paintings that hung in the gallery, but he did not have the patience required to become a successful painter himself.

When he walks through the door, instant reminders of his childhood flood his mind. The atmosphere is eclectic. Christian music can be heard while his eyes feast on the visual stimulus of the various art and photographs that line the walls.

Connie hears the front door open and shut and gets up from her desk to greet her visitor. "Well, hello Lenny. Welcome to my gallery."

Lenny instantly recognizes Connie and returns the greeting. "Hello. I should have known that this was your place. You project the same artistic aura that my mother possesses."

"Well thank you," Connie replies. "I'll let you look around. Let me know if there is anything you like."

Lenny does just that. He circles the room and looks at the wide variety of items on display. Much of the artwork is to his liking, but one piece stops him in his tracks. The picture of the white church with the sunset reflecting in the window captures his eye. He is totally mesmerized with the picture. It is labeled *Jesus Clouds*. This amazing picture captures the beauty of what he wants to remember most about South Haven; the white church, the beach, the lake and the spectacular sunsets. The white church also reminds him of the awesome people who make up this particular church.

Lenny gets Connie's attention and points at the *Jesus Clouds* painting and says, "I want that one."

Connie smiles and yells out to Mickey, "Mickey can you come to the register and help me with this sale?"

Mickey comes to the counter, sees Lenny and greets him with her customary smile. "Hello Lenny, which one did you want?"

Once again, Lenny points at the *Jesus Clouds* painting. Mickey's eyes about pop out of her head and she stammers, "You want the painting and not one of the prints?"

Lenny quickly replies, "I want the painting."

Mickey gulps and says, "That will be $3000.00."

Without even blinking, Lenny digs out a roll of hundred dollar bills big enough to choke a mule. He places thirty of them on the counter. He then asks, "I came on my Harley, could I trouble you with bringing the painting to my houseboat?"

Mickey's smile is on high beam and she about shouts at Lenny, "No problem, no problem at all."

Connie is all smiles and whispers a silent prayer, "Thank you, Lord!" Mickey's missionary trip is now one hundred percent funded and she also has the means to bless a second person. God is good!

Chapter 30

Anxiety is a strong emotion. Many people take medication due to an inability of coping with it. Josie has been absolutely dreading what she needs to do next. She must inform Jerrid that she is pregnant with his unplanned child. She knows that having a child is not even on his radar at this point in his life.

Josie has developed a bad case of self-doubt so she is assuming that Jerrid doesn't even want her anymore let alone her and a crying baby. A hundred worst case scenarios have developed in her mind. She can't think of one single scenario in which being pregnant at her age could be a good thing.

Josie texts Jerrid and ask him if she can come over. Jerrid replies "Yes." He realizes that Josie has been pulling away but he is unsure why. He tells himself, "It's probably just mushy girl stuff." After all he hasn't expected their relationship to go beyond the summer. He plays football and goes to school in Ann Arbor and she plays volleyball and attends school in Kalamazoo. He likes Josie, but thinking of the future is a foreign concept to him. The only future that he can picture consists of playing in front of 100,000 cheering fans. He also entertains the lofty goal of playing in the National Football League.

When Josie gets to Jerrid's place, she doesn't even have to knock. Jerrid is waiting at the door and welcomes her with a hug. He leads her through the guest house and out to the pool. Jerrid's mind starts thinking about sex. It's been a little while since he has had sex with her. However, he did just have sex with the Sea Doo chick.

Josie takes a seat on the diving board and dips her toes into the water. Jerrid is shirtless and only wearing his swimming shorts. He dives into the water and surfaces near Josie. He can tell that something is weighing heavy on her mind so he stretches his muscular arms along the side of the pool while his body bobs underneath him in the water and asks, "What's up?"

Josie stares at her toes and realizes that the paint on her toe nails is in drastic need of a new coat. Normally she is very astute to such matters, but her wandering mind has lost sight of life's little details. She forces herself to look over at Jerrid who is utterly casual and seems totally indifferent. She thinks to herself, "Boy, I'm going to rock his world".

Josie looks back at her toes and starts to speak. "I think that I love volleyball as much as you love football. We both have been dreaming about having our best season ever this upcoming fall. We've both earned the title of Team Captain and have high expectations. One of the opportunities that comes with leadership is the knowledge that so many people are looking to us to do the right thing and to help them achieve personal success through our guidance. You will soon have ten teammates staring you in the face during each huddle to listen for direction. More than likely you will lead your teammates to a championship season, and you will get a rush like no other that will make you feel like you are the king of the freaking mountain! Unfortunately, I won't be feeling that rush this fall. My teammates won't be looking into my eyes for guidance. Instead, they will be led by someone other than me. Because of some poor life choices, I will now be watching from the sidelines thinking what if?"

Jerrid squints his eyes and is trying to decipher where Josie is going with this rambling rant. Why wouldn't she be playing volleyball? That doesn't even make sense.

Josie looks over at Jerrid and realizes that she is just prolonging what she came over to say and in the process has totally confused him. She then stares him in the eyes and blurts out. "What I came over to tell you is I'm pregnant! You are definitely the father and I thought that you should know."

A large lump forms in Josie's throat and with each ticking second of silence the lump only grows. Jerrid's eyes widened when he hears the *"p"* word and he is shocked. Words elude him, and he remains in the pool not knowing what to say. When the silence becomes awkward, Josie gets up to leave. Before exiting the gate she looks back one more time at Jerrid who is still staring at the water. Josie runs to her car and drives away with tears running down her cheeks. Jerrid's total indifference hurts more than she could have ever imagined.

Chapter 31

South Haven is always a popular place, but it becomes even more so during the first week of August. That's when the annual Blueberry Festival occurs. Over 50,000 people visit the small town for this yearly party. A volleyball tournament is scheduled for that weekend, and the girls once again have high expectations.

Unfortunately, Josie is having a rough time with her pregnancy. She experiences morning sickness on a daily basis and often cramps up during the day. Two weeks before the tournament, she approaches Mickey for another talk. This time Josie is much more composed and rather matter of fact with what she needs to say. "Mickey, even though it's still early in my pregnancy and the doctor says that I can still exercise, playing competitive volleyball is just too much. I think that you need to partner up with Stephanie for the Blueberry Festival. She has been great during workouts and she deserves a shot. Teaming with you is the best thing that we can do for her right now. What do you say?"

Mickey should have seen this coming but she hadn't. Listening to Josie's words makes the pregnancy all the more real. She now realizes just how much her friend is going to have to give up. Reality sets in and she nods her head in agreement.

Josie smiles and says, "I'm going to be ok. Let's call Stephanie and let her know."

Mickey places the call to her young friend and says, "Hey Steph, I'm here with Josie and we have you on speaker phone. Josie has something that she wants to ask you."

Josie chimes in, "Hey Steph, will you do me a favor? Will you take my place in the upcoming Blueberry Festival volleyball tournament? I need to take some time off and would love to watch you and Mickey kick some butt. What do you say?"

Stephanie can't hide her joy and practically screams out her reply, "Yes, Yes, Yes. Thank you. I'm so excited!"

Mickey speaks up, "Well then, we will see you in about an hour for practice."

Stephanie quickly replies, "I'll be there, thank you, thank you so much!!!"

After they hang up with Stephanie, Mickey looks at her friend and gives her a big hug. As they embrace Mickey says, "You're awesome."

Josie is actually smiling and says, "I like Stephanie, let's work her hard and get you two a championship win!"

******

Once again Lenny rides his Harley into Kalamazoo. Over a super-slam Denny's breakfast he shares the latest surveillance information to his fellow DEA agent. The heroin smugglers have decided to have Rowdy make his delivery on Saturday during the blueberry festival. Their theory is that law enforcement personnel will be tied up with crowd control and petty disturbances so they will be able to slip in amongst all the boaters enjoying the summer festivities.

The DEA's plan is the same as last time. They will make the bust at the marina after the boat has been safely secured to the dock. Five agents will be working undercover around the marina posing as tourists. Two other agents will be hidden in a van parked in the marina parking lot. Two agents disguised as fisherman will be in a boat parked close to Rob's rental slip. Lenny will patrol the water on a Sea-Doo. If Rob thinks life has been rough the last couple of weeks, just wait until the hammer falls and he is caught holding a large shipment of illegal drugs. You just can't fix stupid.

Chapter 32

A few early morning joggers mixed with a couple of elderly walkers use the south pier for their morning fitness rituals. Lenny, dressed in shorts and a t-shirt, does the same. He notices *The Wolverine* slowly navigating The Black River. Jack sees him and they wave at each other. Jerrid is talking to his morning clients and they all wave as well. The big water is like mirrored glass. The only ripples are the ones caused by the accelerating boats as they roar out into the big blue lake.

Five minutes later, another boat comes through. This one is being steered by Rowdy Rob who is looking rather subdued at this early hour. The self-centered partier rarely awakens before noon, so he is not yet fully awake. Lenny texts his fellow agents that Rob is headed their way. Agents in Chicago plan on taking photographs to document the illegal activity. A lot can go wrong during one of these operations. Lenny is confident that they will get the job done, but only time will tell.

****

While Lenny is monitoring the boats from the pier, Mickey and Stephanie are registering for the beach volleyball tournament. Mickey is optimistically cautious about their chances of winning the title, while Stephanie is giddy with high hopes. If Stephanie stays focused and plays at the level that she is capable of playing, then the girls have a realistic chance of winning. Her lack of experience is definitely a factor, but Josie has agreed to coach and mentor her throughout the competition.

The girls first match starts at 9 a.m. Stephanie is amped up and hits a couple of her hits out of bounds. The score is closer than it should be considering the competition. She settles down nicely in the second game and the girls easily beat their competitors 21 – 7. Josie gives Stephanie a positive pep talk in between games, and the results are fantastic. Josie tells her, "You got this; stay focused and snap your wrist when hitting. If you do that we will win this tournament. I have faith in you!"

****

Jack and Jerrid have Fred and Louann Warden on today's charter. They live in South Haven in the summer and Florida during the winter. If the fish cooperate it could possibly be a quick trip because they only have to serve two anglers instead of the customary four. Each of them can catch a limit of five fish. Ten fish will more than likely utilize most of their strength at this stage of their life.

The first strike of the day is handled by Fred and he quickly grabs the pole out of the holder and sets the hook. A big steelhead jumps out of the water. Sunlight shines brightly on the silver fish illuminating it as it dances on the water. Twenty minutes later Jerrid dips the big net into the water and lifts the heavy fish aboard. He hands the fish to the happy gentlemen, and his wife already has her camera ready to snap a couple of quick photographs. Jack glances at Jerrid with raised eyebrows indicating that he is impressed with the size of the trophy fish. It is easily the biggest one that they have caught. Louanne admires Fred's fish and suggests, "You've talked about getting one mounted for the last ten years. If there was ever a fish to get mounted, I think that this would be the one."

Fred looks at his trophy catch and nods his head in agreement. "Honey, I think you're right. I'm going to do it. He will look fantastic hung over the mantel in our cottage."

****

Meanwhile, Rob follows his Global Positioning System and successfully makes it to the slip at the Chicago marina. A beautiful woman is waiting for him wearing a silk tank top and short white shorts. A barbed wire tattoo circles her tanned right bicep. Her accessories include big gold hooped earrings a gold Rolex watch and a diamond studded gold bracelet. Another diamond stud is pierced on the side of her nose. She has an oversized Coach purse which contains two bricks of Heroin. A brick is a kilo, and after cutting it down it will have a street value of $2,000,000. Rob's looking to clear $50 grand for his day's work. In his delusional mind he feels like a rock star!

The lady boards the boat and without wasting any time Rob heads back out for open water and a return voyage to the marina in South Haven. By now Rob is awake and he eyes the beautiful woman. She is in remarkably good shape. Her legs and arms have muscular definition and she looks like she lives the life of a gym rat.

Too young and dumb to know better, Rob lamely attempts to impress the lady with his wit and supposed charm. Although speech remains difficult, Rob lamely asks, "What's your name or should I just call you beautiful?"

The lady is much wiser in the ways of the world than this young party boy, so she raises her eye brows and throws him a casual glance and says, "Seriously, that's the best you got. "

She then quickly puts him in his place. "Look here, Sport. This is business. We've got a simple little job to do. We take what I have in this bag and carry it across this oversized pond to your little hick town. I then catch a ride with a friend back to Chicago and I never see you again. So stay on task and don't worry about me. It is as if we have never met!"

She then struts into the cabin leaving Rob all alone to drive the big boat back to Michigan. Rob cusses under his breath. He glances into the cabin and sees her lighting up a cigarette. His jaw is healing but the pain still lingers. He now has a throbbing headache and is *jonesin* for a beer; but he was given strict orders to not have any alcohol on the boat while doing this job and for once in his life, he followed a rule. This hasn't been nearly as adventurous as he originally thought. Being treated like a peon doesn't sit well with the cocky hothead. This summer has been one major buzzkill.

Chapter 33

The ball sizzles over the net right at the tired high school athlete. Stephanie bends her knees and successfully passes the jump serve to Mickey. Her stellar teammate once again sets the ball perfectly for her to slam it over the net. Setting her feet, Stephanie springs high in the air and throws her right arm forward. Determined and focused, her timing is perfect and she drives the ball violently downward towards the left out of bounds line. Picture perfect, the ball lands two inches in bounds, just out of the reach of the diving Penn State player who is contending from the opposite court. The game is tied 20 - 20! Mickey calls a timeout.

The girls walk to the sideline and Josie throws them each a towel to wipe off their sweat. Stephanie looks tired, yet determined. Josie praises her last play. She then looks her in the eye and says, "I can see that you are tired but you've got to remain hungry. They are tired too, and it's time for you to finish this with your jump serve. Serve it towards the blond's left arm. I guarantee you that she will at least hit the first one out of bounds if you put enough heat into it. I have faith in you. Are you ready?"

Stephanie nods her head and takes a big drink of water. Her eyes indicate that she is focused. She has that same killer instinct that Mickey and Josie have. She can smell the victory and is determined to finish strong!

The girls walk back out onto the court and the referee tosses Stephanie the ball. Stephanie steps back behind the serving line. She takes a big breath and exhales air. She tosses the ball high into the air, jumps up, and delivers a hard blow that rockets the ball over the net. The serve is aimed perfectly in the direction that Josie instructed, and the opponent barely gets her arms on the serve when the ball deflects out of bounds.

Stephanie looks over to Josie and she mouths "same thing for the win!" Stephanie rears back and serves a carbon copy of the previous serve and gets the exact same result.

That point gives the girls a two point win in the deciding game of the tournament, and they have successfully won the championship match in Stephanie's inaugural outing. Stunned beyond belief, Stephanie's eyes bulge wide open as she victoriously raises her hands in the air and rushes to embrace her talented teammate. Mickey embraces her younger friend, and they jubilantly jump up and down. Josie stands on the sideline clapping right along with the large crowd of volleyball enthusiast. Mickey looks over at her friend and waves her onto the court. The three girls embrace and at this very moment all is right in the world.

The girls break their embrace long enough to shake hands with the runner-ups, and then they return to center court and once again do a three way hug. Mickey looks her companions in the eyes and says, "Let's give thanks."

The girls bow their heads and Mickey leads her friends in prayer. "Father in heaven, we thank you for blessing us with solid friendships, good health, and gifting us our talents and abilities. You are a Great God and we thank you for our success, Amen!"

The girls let out a victorious cheer. Mickey and Stephanie walk over to the podium to receive their championship medals. Stephanie looks like a tall drink of sunshine. Josie is very proud of her. She accepts instructions well and overcame her inexperience with grit and determination.

Josie had thought that it might be hard to watch the girls play without her, but she has discovered that she enjoys coaching and feels that she is also pretty good at it. Maybe the upcoming collegiate season won't be a total wash. Maybe she can stay with the team as a player coach. Talk about making lemonade out of lemons.

The local media snaps photographs and approach's the girls for interviews. Stephanie is standing tall. She is quick to point out that her success today came about through the great coaching that she received from Josie and Mickey. She also gives thanks to God and her church family for their encouragement and support. Living a life of substance rather than a life of substance abuse is rewarding! It's never too late to turn your life around, and Stephanie is a living, breathing example. Her story will now be told to thousands of people and serve as an inspiration to others!

Chapter 34

The elderly Warden couple is relaxing in the rear of the boat after a full morning of fishing. They look exhausted after landing their limit of salmon and lake trout. The Wardens lounge on deck chairs as the boat cruises towards shore. Jack notices Mr. Warden rubbing the left side of his chest. Jack asks him, "Mr. Warden, are you alright? I notice that you are massaging your chest." With this being said, Mrs. Warden awakens and bolts upright in her seat.

Mr. Warden attempts to respond but finds himself short of breath. Fred thought that he had strained a chest muscle fighting the big fish but now he is not sure. Mrs. Warden recognizes the symptoms of a heart attack and instructs Jack to call for help.

Jack calls in the emergency over the radio and arranges for medical care to meet them at the dock. The dispatcher calls the bridge operator informing him to open the bridge as soon as the ambulance crosses so that there is no delay in getting the elderly gentleman the care he needs. Mrs. Warden fetches an aspirin from her purse and helps her husband by placing it in his mouth as well as giving him water to drink. Although prayer is a new concept for Jack, he silently asks God, "Help Mr. Warden make it through this ordeal and help Mrs. Warden during this difficult time!"

As *The Wolverine* enters the mouth of the Black River, an ambulance and police car rush to the marina with their lights and sirens on, clearing the route. The DEA agents are none too pleased to see a police car with flashing lights approaching the location of their ambush.

Mr. Murphy from Murphy's Law is their worst agent.
Murphy's Law states, "Anything that can go wrong, will
go wrong!" Once again this proves to be the case.

Emergency personnel rush the dock as *The
Wolverine* eases into the boat slip. Jerrid leaps from the
boat and quickly secures it to the dock allowing
paramedics a safe entry onto the vessel. The emergency
professionals tend to Mr. Warden and they soon have
him strapped to their gurney and transport him to the
ambulance. They believe that it is actually just heartburn,
but they want to make sure of their diagnosis and choose
to take him to the hospital.

As they are loading Mr. Warden into the ambulance,
Rowdy's boat comes into view. Rowdy notices the
flashing lights and his own heart starts to beat rapidly.
He doesn't see the ambulance, but he does see the police
car and his paranoia sets in and he convinces himself that
the police are there for him.

When the ambulance leaves, the police officer stays
behind to get a report from Jack and Jerrid. Jack tells him
the Warden's chartered the boat and Mr. Warden started
displaying signs of a heart attack while they were
cruising back. The officer then casually asks about Rob.
Naturally, he has heard about the kid causing trouble and
was curious what his fellow U of M athletes thought of
him. "I hear that another U of M athlete has a boat down
here. Which one is it?" asks the officer.

Jerrid starts to tell him that it's not here when he
notices Rowdy's boat coming in their direction. Jerrid
points out the boat to the officer. Rowdy sees Jerrid

pointing his boat out to the police officer and starts to panic.

They are currently in a position where turning around is not an option, and yet Rob doesn't dare enter the slip with the drugs on board his boat while the police are sitting there waiting for him. What is he to do?

Impulsively, he formulates a quick plan. On the opposite side of the channel there is a Sea-Doo. Rob takes the two bricks of heroin and places them in a backpack. He then steers the boat towards the opposite bank where he can jump onto the Sea-Doo. He tells Miss Chicago to take the boat over to the slip. Without the drugs there won't be anything they can do to her. Miss Chicago reluctantly agrees since it is the only way that she can foresee avoiding being locked up. After all, she has prior convictions and would be looking at serious prison time if caught.

The large boat hides Rob's movements from the DEA agents, so they don't initially see him boarding the Sea-Doo. When the DEA agents see Rob racing back up the canal they radio Lenny who is on his own Sea-Doo.

Lenny sees Rob and pursues the fleeing perpetrator. Rob quickly notices the approaching rider and guns the throttle. Lenny does the same and the chase is on. Rob is driving recklessly and is petrified about getting caught with such a large quantity of drugs. He had foolishly dismissed any thought of getting caught when planning the run, but now the reality slaps him hard in the face. If caught, he will definitely go to prison. Daddy's attorneys are good, but not that good!

Rob starts to pull away because of several risky moves. He just misses striking two sail boats but manages to stay afloat racing full steam ahead. His adrenaline kicks in and he starts to believe that he will get away. Lenny still has him in sight, but he falls behind not wanting to jeopardize any of the other people using the river. When Rob re-enters the area between the two piers, he glances over his shoulder to find out what kind of lead he has developed before entering the open water. As he does, he drives too close to shore and hits a submerged boulder. Rob is instantly thrown off the Sea-Doo and flies through the air, crashing onto the jagged boulders that line the pier.

Rowdy Rob's body tumbles on the rocks until it lands on top of an extra-large stone that has a flat surface. Blood oozes from his head and his broken femur cuts open the artery in his leg. Hope is a word associated with the living. Rob is no longer of this world.

Lenny finds the backpack filled with heroin lying near Rob's dead body. Several people rush the piers from both North and South Beaches to see what happened. What they find is too much for many of them to stomach.

Back at the marina, Miss Chicago panics and throttles the boat forward and accelerates into *The Wolverine*. Jack and Jerrid helplessly watch as the boat crashes into their fishing vessel. A large hole opens up on their boat and water starts pouring in. Agents board Rob's boat, apprehend the lady from Chicago and conduct a search. Rob had one of his dad's pistols on board and they charge the lady for being a felon in possession of a firearm. She loudly protests and displays a nasty disposition. Her outer appearance would portray a pretty woman, but the words that flow from her mouth testify to the ugliness of her blackened heart.

Lenny radios the news of Rob's death back to the agents at the marina. Jack and Jerrid can hear the conversation and are stunned. It was just a few minutes ago that they saw Rob speeding down the river and within that short amount of time his life has ended.

Rob was a guy who appeared to have it all. He was good looking, athletic and a highly skilled basketball player. His family was wealthy and he seemed to have everything that you could ask for. He lived in a mansion, with full access to cars, motorcycles, a pool and the boat. Unfortunately, he was also intrigued by the lifestyle of the drug culture. Experts refer to this phenomenon as the "high of the buy.'

Jack instantly thinks of a Bible verse that he had read earlier in the week. The verse was in the book of Mark and it read, "What good is it for someone to gain the whole world, yet forfeit their soul?"

Chapter 35

Wow, did that really just happen? Jack and Jerrid ride home in silence contemplating their thoughts. Rob is dead, and it happened so fast. Jack didn't even like Rob, but he is still in shock with the fact that he is gone. All he can think is, "What a waste." The kid had it all and yet he wasn't happy. Rob was chasing after the ultimate high and he could never quench that irrational thirst. The world is full of these stories, but to see it played out so vividly, leaves him feeling numb and disgusted. Right now, he is feeling extremely thankful for his own father who made him promise that he would not touch a drop of alcohol. "But for the grace of God, there go I".

Jerrid is also thinking about Rob's death but in much different terms. In contrast, Jerrid finds himself thinking, "Good riddance." After all, the jerk tried to force himself on Josie.

As soon as they get back to their summer pad, Jerrid makes a bee-line for the fridge and pops the top of a cold beer. He practically has that one drained by the time Jack makes it inside. Jack has seen enough self-inflicted damage for one day so he finally calls his friend out, "Dude, what are you doing?"

Jerrid gives Jack a disgusted look and responds, "What's it look like, I'm drinking a beer."

Jack shakes his head in bewilderment and says, "Yea, you have been drinking beer all summer. You drink too much! Do you want to end up like Rob?"

Jerrid is instantly defensive and thinks to himself, "Oh, you want to go there do you?" He then responds,

"Don't worry about me, it sounds like someone needs to get some. What are you doing dating a virgin? We're in a beach town for crying out loud. Get laid! After all, isn't that one of the reasons why we chose to work here for the summer?"

Jack is momentarily speechless. Jerrid just doesn't get it. He's not as hard-hearted as Rob, but his alcohol dependency has him only thinking of himself. He bites his tongue for a moment but then he decides to go all in.

"Let me get this straight, your advice for me is to get laid. I find that strange coming from someone who just got a girl pregnant. When were you going to bring that fact up?"

Jerrid blurts out a quick retort, "Yeah, Josie's pregnant, so what. I don't know for sure that it's mine. It didn't take a lot of effort to get her to have sex with me. Who's to say that she hasn't had sex with other guys as well? Football starts in another week. I don't have time to think about this right now. She knew what she was doing. If it is mine, then she probably got pregnant because she knows that I have a future in the NFL and is looking for a big payday. Beside the point, what business is it of yours?"

Jack turns around and starts for the door. After he opens it up he turns back around and looks at Jerrid as his friend opens his second beer. "Jerrid, you have been my best friend for many years now. I'm going to tell you straight up. You need help. Get yourself into rehab or it's going to catch up with you. Take it for what it's worth." Jack turns and goes out the door.

****

Jack exchanges texts with Mickey and finds out that she is still at the beach. Jack texts back that he is on his way there. It's been a rough day and he needs to see his girl. When he gets to North Beach he notices someone pulling out of a parking spot right in front of the volleyball area and takes their now vacant spot. Mickey notices Jack as he is getting out of his jeep and runs up to him and jumps up into his arms. What a great feeling to get greeted so enthusiastically. Jack holds her tight and says, "It is so good to see you!"

Mickey releases her embrace and starts reliving the tournament by highlighting Stephanie's achievements in her narrative. The proud high school athlete looks on beaming with pride. Josie looks content as well so he chooses to not even bring up the conversation that he just had with Jerrid.

Jack congratulates all three girls for the tournament win and announces, "This calls for a celebration. Ice cream for everyone, I'm buying."

As they walk the short distance to the ice cream stand, Mickey mockingly teases, "Wow, big spender."

After everyone receives their order, Mickey suggests having a bon fire and invites Josie and Stephanie too. Stephanie jumps at the suggestion and Josie throws her hands into the air and declares, "Why not, I don't have anything else to do."

Mickey tosses her keys to Josie and asks her to drive Stephanie to Connie's so that she can ride with her man. Jack jumps into the driver's seat and yells at Mickey, "Get in sunshine!"

Mickey asks him why he called her sunshine and he replies through a cheesy smile, "Because you brighten my day."

Mickey brightens everyone's day that comes in contact with her. She is pure gold, and Jack is proud of the fact that she called him "her man." Living life right definitely has its rewards. Mickey wouldn't be with him otherwise. Jack wants to continue being the man that the Lord wants him to be.

Chapter 36

Jack rises early Sunday morning to go for a run on the beach. Football season is just around the corner and maintaining his endurance is very important. Running in the sand has also proven to be highly effective at strengthening his legs. Jack enjoys running the beach in the morning. He doesn't even take any music because he loves to hear the sound of the waves splashing ashore. Running also helps to clear his mind of any drama or clutter that is not positive. On this run, his mind is on Mickey and the God that they both serve. This summer has literally been a life changing experience.

When Jack arrives back home he finds that Jerrid has gotten out of bed and is waiting on him. Jerrid's suitcase is packed and resting next to the door. Jerrid is sitting at the table and asks Jack to sit across from him. Jerrid's eyes are red from lack of sleep and his hands are visibly shaking.

Jerrid looks his long-time friend directly in the eye and says, "Jack, I'm sorry for what I said. You're right, I do have a problem. I haven't had a drink since our argument and look how my hands shake. I appreciate you being a strong enough friend and having the guts to tell me straight up. I called coach and told him that I will be a little late for summer practice. My mom is on her way here, and she is going to take me to a rehabilitation center. You're right, I'm not the monster that Rob turned out to be, but at the same time I'm not doing myself or anyone who is around me any favors being drunk all the time."

Jerrid hesitates for a moment and then continues, "Jack, I can see that you have changed. I don't know much about this whole God thing, but I think that it's something, that I need to check out as well. The rehab center is faith based and I plan on learning as much about Him that I can while I'm there. I don't want to be the person that I have become. I will soon have a child coming into this world and I haven't even pursued the relationship with Josie once I found out she was pregnant."

At this point a car pulls up and it's Jerrid's mom. Jack walks his friend out to the car and gives his friend a firm handshake followed up by a manly hug. "I'll be praying for you."

Jerrid nods his head and gets into his mom's vehicle. Jack watches the car drive away until it disappears.

******

Today is Jack's last Sunday in South Haven before heading to school for football practice. Naturally, Jack is sitting beside his beautiful girlfriend in the second row at the Lakeshore Community Church. Today's message is on the ministry of John the Baptist and the preacher encourages everyone who has not been baptized to sign up for a baptism to be held this evening in Lake Michigan.

After the sermon, Jack signs his name and is pleased to see Stephanie's name on the list as well. Before he can set the pen down, Josie walks up behind him and asks for it so that she can sign up. Mickey leans in as whispers into Jack's ear, "Josie rededicated her life to God last night after meeting privately with the reverend."

Jack turns around and observes Lenny on stage putting his guitar in its case. Jack walks up to the stage and Lenny greets him with a handshake. Jack has a favor to ask. "Lenny, I have signed up to get baptized tonigh,t and I would like you to do it. What do you say?"

Without hesitation, Lenny replies, "Brother, I would be honored to."

Jack thanks him and starts to walk away but Lenny has something more to say. "Jack, my name is not really Lenny, its Noah. I am really an undercover DEA agent and Lenny is my cover name. I am here on business. I was the agent who was following Rob on the Sea-Doo when he crashed. I will be leaving next week. I just want you to know one thing that has been true about my time in South Haven. I really am a Christian and I chose to attend this church. Since you have honored me by asking me to baptize you, I find it important to tell you the whole truth."

What Lenny has told Jack is pretty heavy stuff so it takes a moment for it all to settle in. Jack asks, "Was the part about you being a soldier overseas correct?"

Lenny nods his head yes, "That part is true as well. I served three tours overseas and looked evil dead in the eye. That's why I am so grateful that there is a God of love who is the complete opposite of the very evil that I observed."

Jack appreciates another confirmation of faith from the veteran and says, "Well, I'll see you tonight, Noah!"

Chapter 37

Thick billowy clouds loom over the lake. Even though seven o'clock is still considered early in the evening, the famous South Haven sun remains hidden behind the wall of grey and white darkness that engulfs the area. Ten people have signed up for the baptism service, and three of them are here through the strong Christian example that Mickey displays on a daily basis.

Stephanie's father baptizes the first seven, and then he performs the task for his beautiful teenage daughter. Tears form in his eyes and his voice cracks a little as he says, "I now baptize you in the name of the Father, the Son and the Holy Spirit." With that being said, the Reverend submerges his precious daughter under the healing water.

Stephanie emerges clothed in God's grace. She gives her dad a prolonged hug and then walks to the water's edge where she hugs her mother. When she finishes hugging mom, she embraces both Mickey and Josie. There is not a dry eye in the crowd.

After hugging Stephanie, Mickey and Josie wade out into the lake. Mickey has the privilege of dunking her best friend under the water and reciting the same passage the reverend has repeated for the other eight people. Aunt Connie operates her ever present camera and snaps photographs as Mickey says, "I now baptize you in the name of the Father, and the Son and the Holy Spirit."

Josie goes under the water and emerges renewed. She feels God's powerful strength. Connie captures a powerful image of Mickey lifting Josie from the water grave with water droplets flying through the air. When

Josie surfaces, she hugs her best friend and cries tears of gratitude. The church congregation kindly applauds.

Last but not least, is the baptism of Jack Thayer. The muscular men wade out in the water, and as they do an opening develops in the sky. Jesus Clouds allow a bright ray of sunlight through the grey barriers and the bright light illuminates the shoreline. Noah recites the same words used by the reverend and Mickey as he dunks Jack under the water. "I now baptize you in the name of the Father, the Son and the Holy Spirit." The water droplets sparkle as they fly through the air when Jack surfaces. Jack feels invigorated and pumps Noah's hand in a celebratory manner.

Sunlight dances on the water and the congregation knows that God has blessed this event. Mickey runs back into the water and embraces her man. Jack holds her tight and tells her for the very first time, "I love you."

Mickey replies, "I love you too!" She is performing the incredible achievement of smiling and crying at the same time. Connie is having trouble looking through the view finder of her camera because tears have welled up in her own eyes.

As Noah, Jack and Mickey walk towards the shore, Noah stops dead in his tracks. Noah stares up onto the bluff with an astonished expression. He then points towards the church. The painting that he bought from Mickey is now displayed in real life; in vivid color. Once again the church windows are ablaze with the bright light cast out by the setting sun which is filtering through the Jesus Clouds.

Jack holds Mickey's hand as they walk ashore. He turns and says, "What a great ending to a wonderful summer."

Aunt Connie gathers Mickey and her friends together on the beach and presents them each with a brand new customized sweatshirt. Mickey, Jack, Noah, Josie and Stephanie slip on their gifts and are pleased with what is says. "I spent my summer just SOUTH of HEAVEN in South Haven, Michigan!"

Readers Guide

Questions for Discussion

Characters: Mickey McPherson, Jack Thayer, Josie Jones, Jerrid Stone, Stephanie Newhouse, Rob "Rowdy" Bailey, Lenny "Noah" Sanders, Aunt Connie.

1. Which character do you relate to the most?
2. Which characters do you believe will live a life of substance in the future?
3. Which character is most likely to live a life of substance abuse?
4. Marijuana is referred to as a *gateway drug*. Explain this concept and do you believe it to be true?
5. Do you believe that God has the power to change lives?
6. Jack is drawn to Mickey's devotion to her faith in God. Do you believe that a person can have that kind of influence on another in real life?
7. What word best describes Mickey's character?
8. Do you believe that a person's environment affects their personal development?
9. Give examples of how the characters personal background led to good or bad decisions?
10. How influential do you think a person's family history is towards character development?
11. Mickey quotes 1 John 3:7 and states that she does not want to lead anyone astray. Do you share her opinion on the topic of drinking alcohol?

12. Which temptations or "forbidden fruits" do you feel are most prevalent in today's society?
13. What are some consequences for engaging in premarital sex?
14. What are some consequences for engaging in drug use?
15. Name a character and give an example of them choosing right over wrong and then name a second character and give an example of them choosing wrong over right.
16. Can a person "right a wrong?"
17. Have you personally seen the negative effects of substance abuse in your family, friends, church or school?
18. How would a premarital pregnancy change your life?
19. How important are friendships or community in your life?
20. What would you enjoy most about living in the *South Heaven* community?

Jerry Lambert

About the Author

Jerry Lambert is an accomplished outdoor writer who has appeared in many outdoor publications including *Outdoor Life, North American Whitetail, The Christian Sportsman, Bear Hunting, Big Buck, Bow & Arrow Hunting, Turkey Country, Woods-N-Water News and Whitetails Unlimited.* His first two books, *Trophy White Tales: A Classic Collection about North America's #1 Game Animal the Whitetail Deer* and *The Hunting Spirit: Hunting Stories filled with Inspiration and Humor* where Amazon Hunting Best Sellers.

In 2016, Lambert released his debut novel, *North of Wrong: A Luke Landry Novel.* Staying true to his outdoor writing roots, the novel is set in the fabled north woods of Michigan's Lower Peninsula. The story features a Sheriff Deputy, Luke Landry, who thrives to live by a code that his father taught him, "A strong moral compass will keep you living a life north of wrong." The young deputy quickly discovers the population of people who fail to live by the code. Marijuana farmers utilize the public woodlands for their illegal activity and their greed leads to murder.

The author is a Michigan native who graduated from Michigan State University. In addition to writing the author has worked in the criminal justice field for 25+ years. He also coaches volleyball at Calhoun Christian School and remains very active with his various outdoor pursuits.

North of Wrong: *A Luke Landry Novel*

When sportsman, Luke Landry, becomes an Algonquian County Sheriff's Deputy, he fulfills two life-long dreams: a job in law enforcement and permanent *Up North* living. He strives to live by a code that his father instilled in him, "A strong moral compass will keep you living a life *north of wrong!*" Deputy Luke Landry quickly discovers the population of people who fail to live by the code. Marijuana farmers infiltrate the public woodlands, and the ruthless outlaws resort to murder. Luke's best friend, a decorated war hero coping with PTSD, becomes a prime suspect along with Mexican gangsters and local thugs. Fortunately for Luke, he is serving under the legendary leadership of Sheriff Sam Stanton; a true tower of power who administers north woods justice!

"Jerry Lambert knows the woods, the law and a good story. Michiganders will especially enjoy this yarn." **Bobby Cole, Author of *The Dummy Line, Moon Underfoot, The Rented Mule* and *Old Money.***

Jerry Lambert has made one of my favorite corners of the world come to life in *North of Wrong*, and with 25 years in criminal justice under his belt, he knows what he's writing about. Our country needs more Luke Landry's driving the rural roads with a moral compass to give direction and an aim to putting criminals where they belong. And if they find time to catch a few trout and bag a turkey along the way, I'll pay to read that, too." *Keith McCafferty, Field & Stream Survival* **editor and author of the Sean Stranahan mystery series. 2016 Spur Award Winner for Best Western with *Crazy Mountain Kiss***

"Jerry Lambert does it again. *Trophy White Tales* and *The Hunting Spirit* introduced us to this writer's compelling story-telling abilities and *North of Wrong* delivers these same attributes in his entertaining debut novel. A fast paced narrative filled with action and adventure. Lambert successfully places your mind in the north woods environment that is filled with breathtaking scenery. Frequent references to Michigan facts and history further enhance the story. Deputy Luke Landry is a compelling character shaped by a strong moral compass that has him striving to live a life north of wrong. I am looking forward the next Luke Landry adventure." *Up North Journal*

CPSIA information can be obtained at www.ICGtesting.com
Printed in the USA
BVOW06s1540080916

460946BV00004B/13/P